Bob Moats

I0567606

Doyle's Quest

Doyle's Quest

For information and address:
Magic 1 Productions
P.O. Box 524, Fraser MI 48026-0524
Website: http://murdernovels.com
Cover by Bob Moats

Bob Moats

Extra special thanks to:

Special thanks to Val Brooks who edited this book
and for her great suggestions.

Thanks to the beta readers Al Norris, Cindy Gross
Valstad, and Susan Houghton.

Thank you to all the people who purchased this book.
I hope you enjoy it as much as I enjoyed writing it for
my faithful readers.

The Jim Richards Family of Readers is listed in the
back of the book.

Doyle's Quest by Bob Moats

Chapter 1

Marge smiled at the well-dressed man standing before her desk. "I am curator for the Wittington Art Gallery on Woodward and I think someone is stealing our pieces and substituting very clever forgeries. I need a private investigator to find the culprit."

Marge looked to Doyle who was sitting at his desk. He nodded to her and said, "Send him to me."

Oscar went back to his desk, after talking with Doyle about building up business. Marge pointed and said for the man to go to Doyle. He walked the short distance to the desk and stood waiting. Doyle got up from his chair and said, "Please have a seat, Mr…?"

"Charles, Walter Charles," the man replied.

Doyle pointed to his client chair and the man went around and sat. Doyle also sat and asked, "Now,

4

Mr. Charles, why do you think someone is stealing from your gallery?"

"I know it's going on. I've had various articles examined and the consensus is, they are fakes. The originals are missing."

"When did you first realize that this was happening?"

"About a week ago. One of our valuable statues was knocked off its pedestal and broke. I saw that the interior of the statue was made of plaster. This statue was not supposed to be plaster, it was supposed to be granite. There was even a weight inside to make the thing heavy, like granite."

"So, you've had more art items examined?" Doyle asked.

"I did, and out of the ten I took in to be examined, nine were fakes. The value of the art work in question was in the thousands of dollars."

"What's your take on how this could happen?"

"I'm not paid to investigate; I'm curator of the gallery. This is why I'm here to hire you."

His statement didn't make it any easier to get an idea of what could have happened. "Of course, that's my job. But it would help to get an idea of where I can start. Do you suspect your employees? Or do you think this could be an outside job? You must have an opinion."

The man hesitated, then said, "I think it was an inside job, as the police would say. One of the employees must be behind this. I can't just fire all our people to stop one thief, so I need your help."

"Well, I'll need to stop by and check out your set-up to get a feel for how the articles could be removed and replaced," Doyle said. "May I have access to the entire building, the gallery and the back areas? I presume you have a shipping dock and storage?"

"Yes, we do, and I'll see you have access to all areas. I have the board of directors to answer to, so I need to get this handled quickly and discreetly."

"I am the epitome of discreet investigators," Doyle said, and noticed that Oscar was holding in a laugh.

"Very well. Come to my office tomorrow morning and I'll give you a tour of the facility. Many of our acquisitions are on loan from friendly countries. It would be very bad if they found their treasures were being pilfered."

"I understand. I'll meet with you in the morning."

"I hate to bring it up, but what about your fees?"

"We charge $200 a day while on the job, five percent recovery fee, and expenses, which we will provide receipts for."

"That sounds reasonable. Considering the cost of our missing articles, you should do well with your recovery fee. I'll see you then." He stood and held out his hand. Doyle took it and they said their goodbyes. On his way to the door, the man nodded to Marge and left the building.

Oscar came rushing over. "Art gallery, and your name is Art, it's karma. Are you going to get one of those hats like Indiana Jones wears?"

"Why would I do that?" Doyle asked.

"Well, you're going to hunt for missing artifacts like Jones did. So you'll need a hat."

"I don't wear hats, other than an occasional baseball cap. And, I'm not Indiana Jones, so don't start spreading that around." Doyle tried not to smile, but he did. "I always liked Jones, maybe I'll see if I can find that hat."

Marge came over. "I know just the place where they have those hats. It's a little shop called Harry the Hatter. My Max used to go there to get his hats. Max looked so good in a hat. You should see if they still carry the Indiana Jones hats."

Doyle started laughing, "I think I'd look silly, but I may take a look and see. I'm not saying I would wear one, but…"

Marge's phone rang and she went back to her desk, sat and answered. "Doyle and Drew Investigations," she said. Doyle decided to give Oscar some credit in the name of the firm. Doyle and Drew had a nice ring to it. "May I help you?" She listened then said, "Hold one minute." She clicked the hold button and turned to Oscar. "You have a Mr. Greenstreet calling about his wife. The one you followed the other day."

"Ah, yes, the wife cheating with his best friend. I'll take the call." Oscar went back to his desk and picked up the phone.

Doyle went to Marge's desk and sat. "Do you think I would look good in one of those Indy hats?"

"You have a well chiseled face, rugged and bold. I think you'd look great."

"I know you're just blowing smoke up my shorts, but thanks. Maybe I'll take a look at them."

"Good, I'll write down the directions to Harry the Hatter. He's been in business for over sixty years. He makes hats for many famous people, too."

"Okay, sounds good," Doyle said as Oscar came over. "You look serious, what's up?"

"That was my client for the cheating wife I followed yesterday. Seems she was murdered last night and he wants me to provide the police with everything I had while I was following her."

"That's privileged, but if he's okay with sharing it, then get it all ready to go. Did he ask if we could investigate the murder?"

"He said the police are investigating, which they should be. I mentioned that an independent investigation may help his case, since he is under suspicion for the murder. He said he'd let us know."

"Good. We just got back from finding a serial killer for no pay, now maybe we'll start getting some income," Doyle said and looked at Marge. "I'd like to pay you better than I have. You deserve it."

"Oh goodness, I'm not worrying about it, just gas money and pay for the coffee, I'm happy," she said with a smile.

"Yeah, we'll work on it. If this gallery has thousands of dollars in articles stolen, we should get a hefty recovery fee. First I have to find out who the thief is, and then recover the stolen goods."

"You may have to travel to Egypt to recover the items. An Indy hat would shade you nicely," Oscar said.

"I doubt I'll have to go further than the streets of Detroit to find the items," Doyle said, then continued, "Marge, order a large pizza with everything from Cloverleaf Pizza and have it delivered. I think we have enough in petty cash to cover it."

"Yes, we do, for one pizza, then petty cash is tapped out."

"I'll have to withdraw a little money from the bank to bolster up the fund."

Marge called to order the pizza, Oscar went to get his files on the murdered wife together, and Doyle stood looking in the mirror on the back wall wondering how he'd look in a hat.

About an hour later, they had their fill of pizza and were sitting around talking. "I called the insurance company about rebuilding my cabin since Skeeter blew it up. They said they're sending an agent to discuss the policy I have. I've kept up the payments, so I'm not worried. I just hope they don't give me a hard time. The insurance agent is supposed to be here after noon."

"Arthur, it is after noon," Marge said, just as the front door opened. In came a woman, around her late thirties, well dressed in a skirt showing nice legs, suit jacket, and carrying a valise. She was very attractive and had shoulder length auburn hair. "I think your insurance agent is here," Marge said, getting up and going to the woman.

"I think your next girlfriend just came in," Oscar grinned and went back to his desk.

Doyle didn't give Marge much of a chance to talk to the woman, he was right there next to them. "Arthur, this lady is from your insurance company. I'll let you two get acquainted." Marge went to her desk and picked up her knitting.

"I'm Poppy Drake, from American Life and Casualty, and I'm here about your cabin."

"Pleasure to meet you Poppy, may I call you Poppy? You can call me Art. Please, come and sit at my desk." He led her there and pulled the client chair closer to his chair. She sat and so did he. They were closely facing each other. She looked slightly uncomfortable, so Doyle pushed his chair back a little.

"So, what do you need to know? My cabin was blown up by a crazed serial killer and it's a wreck. I've had the cabin for almost twenty years, since just before I went into the FBI. I was in a terrorist tactical team." Doyle was starting to babble. He stopped talking and asked her to proceed.

"Thank you. I haven't been to the site of the destruction yet, to evaluate, so I can't say what will need to be done to fix your building."

"Oh, it can't be fixed. It's burnt out pretty good. It'll have to be razed and a new building put up. I'd be more than happy to drive you to the property so you can see it," he said, hoping she would go with him.

"That's all right, I'll have my boyfriend drive me up."

Doyle could hear Oscar snickering.

*

Chapter 2

Doyle smiled and told her, "My associate, Oscar Drew, will be more than happy to draw you a map to the site. He's good at drawing maps for people."

Doyle looked to Oscar and smiled. "Aren't you good at sending people to my cabin, Oscar?"

Oscar grinned, remembering when he sent Val, Doyle's former girlfriend, to the cabin without telling Doyle, and she found a dead body. Doyle wasn't about to let Oscar forget that. "Sure, I can give her directions," Oscar offered.

"Good, I'll let you two confer on the directions. I have to go see a man about a hat." Doyle helped the woman up and led her to Oscar. She stood at his desk until he offered her a seat. Doyle turned and went to Marge.

"I'm feeling like getting a hat," he said.

"Good, you'll look rugged in a nice hat. You have the directions, you should be able to find it."

"I'm sure I will," he said and went to the back door and exited. Doyle drove out and was thinking about Amber, the bartender from up in Oxford, and wondered how she was doing. She was weary from having her life in danger being around him, so she broke it off. He knew he could go visit her every so often, but it was over between them for any long term romance, just pure sex now. Not that he minded, he did have an active libido that needed to be quenched often.

13

Doyle's Quest

He arrived at a small storefront lodged between two larger brick buildings down a side street from Woodward. He lucked out finding a parking spot right in front of the store. The sign said *Harry the Hatter*, so it must be the place. He went to the door and in. There was no one in the room except an older, balding man who stood about five foot nothing.

"Welcome to my establishment, what can I do for you today?" The man had a Yiddish accent, as if he had come right over from the Old Country.

Doyle almost felt embarrassed to ask. He looked around the shop at the dozens of hats hanging from the walls, but didn't see the Indy Jones hat he was interested in.

"You look like a dangerous man, a cop maybe? Or someone in the mob?" He laughed at the statement. "I have a nice felt fedora in black that would set your face off nicely."

Doyle finally spoke, "No, I'm looking for the hat worn by Indiana Jones, from the movies."

"Ha, yes!" he exclaimed with delight. "You would look fantastic in that hat. I have only one left in the back. I'll go get it." He toddled off behind a curtain to the back.

Doyle walked around studying the many hats, from straw to leather. He picked out a nice one that reminded him of the hat that Frank Sinatra wore in his day. He tried it on and looked in a mirror on the wall.

"Scooby-dooby-do," Doyle sang quietly. He heard a noise and put the hat back. The old man came back out with a hat. Doyle recognized it right off. It was the Indy hat. He went to the counter and the man handed it to him. He went back to the mirror, put it on and looked, turning his head from side to side.

"Yes," he said. "I like it. I'll take it. How much?"

The old man said, "For you, it's on the house. You saved our mayor's life, so you are a good guy."

That struck Doyle. His fame was getting ahead of him. "Well, thank you. I'm surprised you recognized me."

"I saw your picture on the TV when it happened. You took the mayor's abuse very well."

"Yeah, he finally apologized for that. We're on good terms now. Thank you for the hat. You were recommended to me by my secretary. Her husband used to buy his hats here."

"What was his name? I never forget names."

Doyle's Quest

"Max Wayne, former cop in Detroit," Doyle replied.

"Ah, yes, your secretary is Margie Wayne, wonderful woman. Tell her Harry said hello, and say I'm sorry to hear of Max's passing."

"I'll tell her, and thank you for the hat, it's perfect. I'll be sure to recommend you."

The old man thanked Doyle as he left. Out on the street, Doyle was feeling good in the hat. Men don't often wear this type of hat, but he was determined to start a trend. Anyone can wear a baseball cap, but it takes a confident man to wear an Indiana Jones fedora.

He got in his car and drove back to his office. He went in the back door and Oscar stood and walked to him. Oscar circled around Doyle, as he stood in the back.

"I like it. You look good, and I'm not just saying that. You look like Harrison Ford as Indy. I knew you looked familiar."

Doyle grinned and went to the front. "Harry said to say hello and gave his condolences for Max."

"Harry was always a good person. Now, you look great in the hat. Very much like Indy. How's it feel?"

"A little odd, but I think I'll get used to it. Now I'll have to get an aviator flight jacket, too." He removed the hat and set it on his desk. "Did you provide the directions to the cabin?" he asked Oscar.

"Yes, I did, and she told me she didn't actually have a boyfriend, she just thought you were coming on too strong. So, she's single and up for grabs if you don't hit on her too strongly."

Doyle smiled and said, "I'll just play it safe and not say anything. If she's interested, she'll come to me."

"Okay, if you say so," Oscar said and went back to his paperwork.

"Heard anything from your client about the murder charges?"

"No, not yet. I'll call him soon to see if he still needs my files."

Doyle went to his desk and sat staring at the hat. He was intrigued by it, something worn by a movie idol. Not that he was an idol, but it may make him look better. Especially to women.

It was getting late and Doyle told Marge and Oscar to go home, then he closed up the office and went home. He had a quiet night and slept well. Early the next morning he went into the office finding Marge and Oscar already in. He greeted them and went to his desk.

The office phone rang and Marge answered. She spoke her usual intro then waited. She put the caller on hold and turned to Doyle. "The curator at the art gallery is on the line. He said they had a murder and he wants you to come right away."

Doyle said he'd take the call, picked up the phone and said, "Mr. Charles, Art Doyle here. You told my secretary that you've had a murder?"

The voice on the phone replied, "Yes, Mr. Doyle, it happened while I was out. I came back and found our art appraiser dead in the preparation room where we have our pieces readied for showing. I called the police and they are all over the place. I need you here to keep an eye on them, please."

"I'll be right over," Doyle said and hung up. He went to Marge, "Got a new wrinkle in the case. I'll be back when I can." He started to go to the back door when Marge called to him to take his hat. Doyle stopped and grinned, went to his desk, lifted the hat and put it on. He tilted it down over one eye and said to Marge, "Watch the place, doll. Don't let any mugs shoot Oscar."

Marge laughed as Doyle headed out. A short time later, Doyle arrived at the gallery. He had never been in the building before, not that he didn't care for art, but he just never had the time. He entered through the front and found a uniform standing by the information counter.

The officer turned to Doyle and said, "Well, if it isn't Doyle, our famous marksman."

Doyle wasn't sure if he should punch the guy or laugh, so he smiled. "Who's in charge?" he asked.

The officer said, "Detective Lowe."

"Harry Lowe?"

"That's him. He should be in the curator's office."

"Thanks," Doyle said and asked where the office was. The officer pointed the way and Doyle went there. He arrived at a door that had the name 'Walter Charles, Gallery Curator' printed on a brass plaque on the wall next to the door. The door was open and he looked in. There were four people in the room, Walter Charles, two men in suits, and Harry Lowe. Lowe had helped Doyle and Oscar when they were trying to find a missing father and Lowe was investigating the murder of a young girl.

Lowe looked to the door and saw Doyle. He waved and went to him. "What are you doing here, Doyle?"

Doyle's Quest

"I was hired by Charles to investigate thefts of art objects. What happened?"

"Still trying to find out. Charles found the body in the back room where they sign in and examine art thingies."

"Art thingies? Is that now the technical term for objects of art?"

"I'm not really impressed by art thingies, I'm more concerned about my own thingies, like my cell phone, tablet, computer, you know, important thingies."

"Ah, you are a real 21st Century Renaissance man. Was it a murder?"

"Looks that way. He was stabbed by some knife they use to examine art thingies. It's used to scrape statues so they can check the content of the scrapings to determine the age of the thingies."

"Can you stop calling them thingies? It sounds weird."

"Okay, fine art, how's that?"

"Better. I know you aren't refined, nor are you a patron of the arts, but you could just pretend."

"Yes, sir. I'll do my best. Now, I need to find out who killed the thingies' appraiser. " He grinned and started to walk away, but stopped. "Nice hat, Doyle, trying out for the next Indiana Jones movie?" Then he went off, snickering.

*

Chapter 3

Doyle felt like throwing a thingie at Lowe, but refrained. He waited by the door as the men in the room finished talking. The two suits left, followed by Lowe, who grinned as he passed Doyle. Doyle reached out and slapped Lowe on the back of the head. Lowe laughed and kept walking away. Doyle turned to the room and entered. Walter Charles was standing by his desk as Doyle came up.

"Mr. Doyle, good of you to come so quickly. It's been a horrible experience finding David dead. He was our best artifact appraiser," Charles said.

"Do you think this could have something to do with the robberies?" Doyle asked.

"You tell me. David was the person I trusted to tell me which art objects were real or fake." He paused, "Okay, I do believe this could have something to do with the robberies. So, I'll need you to get on this as soon as possible. The police will be nosing around even though I haven't told them about the robberies."

"Don't you think that would help with finding the person who killed your man? You're withholding information for their case."

"I understand that, but I don't want the theft of the articles to become public. There are certain powers-that-be here that wouldn't like the articles to be exposed."

"That doesn't make sense. The art works are on display for the public to see, how can they not be exposed?"

"If the police investigate, it may come out as to where the art works originated from," Charles said and sat at his desk.

"Are they stolen by the people who donated them to the gallery?"

"Mr. Doyle, this is sensitive information. We were given these articles on the stipulation that we didn't publicize the ownership. A small gallery like ours wouldn't bring much attention to the art works.

But the exposure of the murder, subsequent revelation of the theft of the articles in question, and their ownership, would be disastrous."

Doyle was having trouble understanding why a person, or persons, would donate their precious art works and not want to be mentioned. If these articles were stolen by the people donating them, then it would be a criminal offense, if they were stolen. The gallery may love to present the articles to the public, but would they risk their reputation to possess stolen goods?

"So, you say that you accept these articles on the stipulation that you don't reveal the ownership? That's a little weird. Do all galleries and museums operate this way?"

"Mr. Doyle, let's say a statue that was once a part of the Byzantine era came into possession of the government of Peru, just saying. Then the statue was taken back by the people of the country it originally belonged to. Would that really be stealing? The artifacts would go back to the proper owners, but the law doesn't see it that way."

"I can see that. This world is based on who has the property in their possession, even if they didn't originally own it. Hitler collected masses of art works, many of which were destroyed to never be seen again. I can understand when our military went in during war time to retrieve the art works to preserve them. I know about that movie, *The Monuments Men* on that subject."

"Yes, those men recovered many articles of importance. We have a small budget to show our pieces, and it is desirable to have people donate articles of great importance to present to the public. We pride ourselves on having a variety of great art works. But the people who donate the articles don't want to be revealed."

"May I, at least, know who these people are? It would help my investigation," Doyle asked.

Charles paused, thinking, then said, "I'll expect you to be very discreet about it. But if you feel it's important to know, I'll tell you."

"Fine, but let's wait until the police are done with their skulking around the building. We can talk later, in private. Who were the two men with the detective?"

"They were from immigration. David wasn't a citizen of the United States. He was a citizen of Egypt, here on a visa to work in the gallery. He was an expert on Egyptian artifacts."

"Why would immigration be interested?"

"They wanted to know why a citizen of a foreign country was murdered in our country. I didn't ask details from them."

Harry Lowe stuck his head back in the door and asked, "Mr. Charles, can you join me for a moment? You can tag along too, Indy." Lowe grinned and went back out.

Doyle would have to get back at him later, he thought, as he followed Charles out of the room. They went down a hallway to a room guarded by uniformed officers. Lowe passed them through and they went into a back room where there were many crates and boxes surrounding a table where the body of the appraiser was slumped over, dead.

"This is how you found the body?" Lowe asked Charles.

"Yes. I came in early to check with David, since he was working to examine some articles, and found him just like this. I went to him to see if he was all right. I didn't touch him, I do know that much, and could see the blood on the table. I went to my office to call the police."

"Nothing in the room was moved or disturbed?" Lowe asked.

"Nothing at all while I was here. There was no one else in the building at the time, I told employees coming in to wait in our break room. Everyone has to punch the clock when they arrive."

"Good, our forensic team will be in shortly. They had other crime scenes to work. My men will be at the door to make sure no one else enters. Including you, Indy." Lowe grinned again.

Doyle grinned back and they left the room, led by Lowe. In the hallway, Lowe turned and asked, "Any suggestions as to why he may have been murdered?"

Charles didn't speak, Doyle answered, "Mr. Charles hired me to find a couple missing items in his gallery, and I presume the killer was the person who took the articles and may have thought the vic might have information."

"What missing items?"

"A couple statues, nothing of importance, except to art lovers. But you wouldn't know about fine art would you, Harry?" Doyle said to distract Lowe.

"You know, I could have you ejected from the crime scene."

"But you won't, because you know I'll just come back. I was hired by Mr. Charles, I'm working for him now."

"Fine, just stay out of the way until we're finished," Lowe said and went off.

"Thank you, Mr. Doyle. I didn't know how to answer his question," Charles said to Doyle.

"Since the police will be here a while, I can't do anything until they finish, so I'll return tomorrow and we can talk more. Just avoid Detective Lowe, he's a good cop but not very much into fine art. You can confuse him with fancy talk about the art works on hand. I can guarantee he'll start avoiding you. I'll see you tomorrow," Doyle said and went down the hall to the exit.

Outside, he found Harry Lowe having a cigarette. "You know those things can kill you."

"So can a bullet, but I have to put up with being shot at numerously. I'll take the slow death any day. So, what is your major function on this?"

"As I said, I was hired to track down a couple of missing statues. It may or may not have to do with the murder. I'm sure you'll figure that out. Charles is a strange bird and has no ideas about crime. He gave me a hard time getting him to explain about the value of the thingies. The stolen items had nothing of real value, not like the crown jewels. But, it's not good for a gallery to have thieves hitting on them."

"Or murderers. If you happen to come across any good info in your investigation, I'd appreciate a nod."

"Sure, you can be my sidekick, Short Round. Even though you're older than the kid."

"You have Oscar to be your sidekick, not some annoying kid from the movie. I have enough troubles without having to follow you around."

"Excuse me, but I have to jump on my horse and chase the evil-doers into the desert to reclaim the treasures they stole," Doyle said, trying not to smile.

"Yeah, see you in the movies, Jones."

Doyle tapped the brim of his hat, turned away, and headed back to his car. He returned to his office and went in to find Poppy Drake sitting next to his desk. He could tell she was looking at his hat. He removed the hat and set it on his desk.

"Well, you are a pleasant sight to see. Did you go to my wreck of a cabin already?" he asked and sat.

"Yes, and I agree, it was totaled. I'm going to recommend rebuilding the cabin," she said. "Do you know any contractors in the area of your cabin that can submit a bid on the job?"

"I'll call a sheriff friend of mine to see if he knows anyone. Do you have a card that I can use to reach you?"

She opened her purse and took out a card. She handed it to him with a smile. "My cell phone number is on the back, if you need it."

Doyle took the card and turned it over. "I'll definitely call, but one question?"

"And that is?"

"Would you consider having dinner with me tonight?"

*

Chapter 4

"I hardly know you, Mr. Doyle," she replied.

"I'm not asking for a relationship, just dinner to celebrate the rebirth of my cabin."

"I'll think about it. Call me in a couple hours and I'll give you an answer." She stood and thanked him, then left.

Doyle's Quest

"I think you may break the ice queen," Oscar said, going over to Doyle.

"Ice queen?"

"Yeah, she's all prim and proper, all business. Can't give you an answer now, has to think on it. She's a little cold, I would say."

"And you base this on your extensive experience with women."

"Hey, I've been through three wives, one of which could freeze the sun with a glance. But knowing you, you'll melt her down."

"Don't you have some case to go on?" Doyle asked.

"As a matter of fact, I do. Another cheating spouse. I think Detroit is full of cheating spouses."

"Yeah, well, they pay and we need the business. Pizzas aren't cheap."

Oscar laughed and went back to his desk. Marge came over to Doyle and asked, "So, how did you like wearing your new hat?"

"I enjoyed it and it was a conversation starter. I'll get used to it. How are you feeling?"

"I'm fine, never been better. What did you find out about the murder?" she asked.

"Not much, the art appraiser for the gallery was the victim. I think it had something to do with the stolen art pieces. The police are overrunning the place, so I'll go back in the morning."

"Do you think Miss Drake will go to dinner with you?"

"Do you listen in on my conversations, too?"

"Well, you took down the partition walls, so it's easy to hear you."

"As a private secretary in a private investigating firm, you are sworn to never repeat anything you hear."

"My lips are sealed. Ever since Val left you to travel the world and you are no longer seeing Amber, you need a new girlfriend. It goes with the P.I. image. Hot women and fast cars. You only have one, now."

Doyle grinned at Marge. She was right, he had to maintain the image. "I'll call her and see if she's brave enough to go to dinner with me."

"Be sure to wear the hat, women go for men in sexy hats."

Doyle's Quest

"I'll remember that," he said as Marge's phone rang. She went to answer.

Doyle sat and waited to see who was on the phone. Marge talked for a couple minutes then hung up. She looked to Doyle and said, "Sorry, it was my sister. She's starting to bug me now that I spent a couple days with her. I should have stayed home and risked having a killer come and get me. It would have been less stressful than staying with my sister. I told her not to call me here again."

"It's okay, Marge, as long as she doesn't interfere with work. Speaking of, I'll probably be busy for a couple days on this gallery case, if Oscar isn't busy, have him take any new cases."

"Sure, dump all the less glamorous cases on me, like chasing spouses," Oscar moaned.

"The next major case of a missing hot babe that comes in, you get it," Doyle said, trying not to laugh.

"That's better," Oscar said and went back to his paperwork.

Doyle stood and went to Marge. "I'm going back to my place and get cleaned up for my hopeful date tonight."

"You'll be fine, Arthur. She won't be able to resist you. Don't forget your hat."

Doyle grinned and said, "We'll see." He turned, picked up his hat and went by Oscar, "You have control, I'm heading out."

"I want proof that you took her back to your place, or hers."

"I'll take pictures," Doyle said and went out the back door.

He spent about an hour in the bathroom, showering and getting ready for his big date. He hoped. This woman would be a challenge for him. As Oscar said, she was a tough one. An ice queen.

He went out to the living room and sat on the couch, staring at his phone and the card she gave him. He had faced crazed criminals and serial killers, so why was this woman scaring him. He was thinking of all the excuses she could come up for not going out with him. She had to wash her hair, the oldest excuse. Or she had laundry to do, the second oldest excuse. Maybe she had two children she had to watch, that would be a killer. He liked kids, but not his date's kids.

"Oh, well, just jump right into it," he said aloud and pushed the buttons on his phone. He waited for a moment when he heard her answer. Good so far, she answered and he heard no children screaming in the background.

"Hello, Poppy Drake here," she said stiffly.

Wow, so formal, he thought. "Poppy, it's Art Doyle. I'm calling to see if you feel like dinner."

"No, I don't feel like dinner, but I feel like *having* dinner," she said and started to laugh. "Are you offering?"

"Uh, yes. I thought I had covered that earlier. Yes, I'm offering you dinner."

"Take out or eat in?" she asked.

"Huh? I'm not sure what you mean."

"Do you want to eat in a restaurant, or get take out and bring it back to my place?"

The ice queen just melted all over the place. "Whatever you want, Poppy. I'm agreeable."

"Good, pick up some Chinese, whatever you like, and come over here. I'll give you the directions."

Doyle was a bit stunned, but took down the directions. What was this woman up to, he wondered? Was his life in danger from a crazed woman? Or was he in for a wild ride?

"I'll see you in an hour. Be ready for a great meal," Doyle said.

"It better be great," she said and laughed. Then she hung up.

Doyle sat back and considered his options. He could go get Chinese, then go into the jaws of death or…well, there was no second option. He stood and went to call the nearest Chinese restaurant and order take out.

Forty-five minutes later, he had three bags of food and was on his way to Poppy Drake's house. He knew the area where she lived. It was a nice neighborhood, middle to high class residents. It was part of the area he had patrolled when he was a uniformed cop so many years ago. He found the building and parked on the street.

He picked up the bags from the passenger seat and went to the front door. It opened before he could knock and there stood Poppy, wearing a tight, short, low cut black dress, high heels, big pearl necklace and a smile.

"Art, good to see you, come on in," she opened the door wider and let him in. He was still wondering what she was up to.

Doyle's Quest

She took the bags from him and went down a hallway to the kitchen. He followed her, watching her nice rear end sway, hugged by the tight dress. She started to empty the bags, putting the small containers into the fridge, as Doyle stood watching her, wondering why.

She was looking good in the dress. It was tight in all the right places and accented her curves. She looked to him, "I'm glad you wore your hat. Indiana Jones, right?"

He tried not to laugh, "Yes, it's the same hat. My secretary thinks it makes me look good."

"Well, she's a smart woman. It does make you look good. You can remove it now."

Doyle realized he still had it on. "I'm sorry, I'm not used to it. I just got it yesterday." He took it off and placed it on a small table nearby with a phone resting on it.

"I'm confused," Doyle said. "Earlier you were a different person, all business. Now you are looking very…well, sexy. I'm getting mixed messages."

She turned to Doyle, "I talked to a number of people up in Oxford, about the incident with your cabin. I had to investigate to get all the facts."

"Of course, you had to be sure I didn't burn the place down myself."

"I'm a good investigator, as I'm sure you are, from what I've heard. One woman was more than happy to talk about you. Amber was her name."

That took Doyle by surprised. "Well, you sure do investigate, don't you?" Doyle inquired, wondering what the two women had to discuss.

"She gave me very detailed information about your adventure with the serial killer and what kind of man you are. I was impressed."

"I just did what I had to do to bring him to justice."

"Yes, I heard about your justice. The killer deserved what he got, didn't he?"

"Well, it's all in my report to the sheriff."

"Yes, I read that report. Your sheriff, Mike Twain, is a friend?"

"We've know each other for a number of years."

"Well, he had a lot to say about you, I'm impressed. Your hat fits you well, Indy."

Doyle's Quest

"I'm not exactly as adventurous as Indy, but I do what I have to do, to solve a case."

She came over to Doyle, standing very close. "I have a mystery I need solved, and you can wear the hat to work on it."

"What's your mystery?" Doyle asked nervously. He never felt this way, and it bothered him to be so at a loss for words and not knowing what to do. He was just going to go with the flow and hope it led to better things.

"My mystery is, how you are going to get me into bed tonight? I may resist and fight, but you'll have to be a big strong P.I. to solve my case." She kissed his cheek and said, "First, let's see if you can solve the mystery of where my bedroom is." Then she went off. Doyle stood long enough to feel stupid and then followed her.

*

Chapter 5

Sometime around three a.m. Doyle was staring at the ceiling of the bedroom. He was amazed by the events of the last seven hours and the amazing change in the woman next to him. Was she a she-demon who wanted to steal his soul? Nah, she was just a woman who wants what she wants, and takes it. He had numerous relations with women in his past, but never one who went from a stern harpy to sexual siren.

Most women he had to deal with were all strong women but he didn't have to work hard to get them where he wanted them. They were all women who were, for a lack of better word, easy women. Now, here he was with Poppy, a tough, no nonsense woman who suddenly became a dynamo from her ice queen persona.

He had to stop thinking about women, it usually got him in trouble. He looked over at her, head on the pillow, so beautiful in the light from the other room. She opened her eyes as if she could hear him thinking. He stiffened.

"Can't sleep?" she asked.

"I'm a light sleeper. The result of my FBI terrorist team training to always be aware of your surroundings."

"What were you thinking?" she asked.

"I was just surprised by the turnaround in our relationship," he replied.

"Relationship? I thought you said you didn't want a relationship."

"That was before," he said.

"Before what?"

"Before you were a strictly business type, but now you're a much better type."

"I know what I want and I wanted you. I was very impressed by what I heard from your friends and associates…and past girlfriends. By the way, she was impressed with your abilities in bed."

"Can we talk about something else?"

She laughed and sat up. "I need a drink of water, I'll be back," she said, and slid out from under the covers. She went out of the room, naked and beautiful. Doyle watched her until she was out.

He reached over and grabbed his phone. He speed-dialed Oscar, and after two rings Oscar came on, "Art, this better be good, I was sleeping."

"I'm calling from the ice queen's bedroom. Just wanted to let you know." He laughed and hung up. He knew Oscar would be up now, thinking about what he said. He shut off the phone so Oscar couldn't call back.

Poppy came back into the bedroom carrying a glass of water and handed it to Doyle, who was sitting up against the headboard. "Thank you, I was a bit parched."

She slid back in and said, "So, did it feel good to brag to your buddy?"

Doyle felt like a deer caught in the headlights, "How did you know about the call?"

"The bathroom is on the other side of that wall and there's an open vent between the rooms. I could hear you."

"You're dangerous. How would you like to come work for me?"

"You couldn't pay me what I'm making now. But I'll consider it if I ever get tired of proving people are cheats and burning down their houses for the insurance." She paused, then said with a smile, "Now we need to discuss this ice queen reference."

"Uh-oh," Doyle said and slid under the covers.

Next morning, Poppy was up and dressed. Doyle was struggling to get his clothes on. He stood and went to the kitchen where Poppy was drinking a cup of coffee. "If you want breakfast, you'll have to make it. I don't eat breakfast."

"Well, it looks like I found my soul mate," Doyle said with a grin. "I don't eat breakfast either. I'll call today to get someone to give you a bid on rebuilding my cabin."

"Well, so much for romantic conversation," she laughed. "I'll expect that call. Now that we're back to ourselves, me, the ice queen and you the horny P.I."

"In my defense, I didn't start that ice queen comment. Oscar did."

"Passing the blame, it's so beneath you. But I'm sure he did. Now, go to work, and so shall I."

They went out to their cars, Poppy gave Doyle a lip lock he wouldn't forget all day. She laughed and went to her car and drove off. He stood watching her leave. "Wow, she is me," he said, and got in his car.

He went in the back door of the office and Oscar turned to him. "I didn't sleep too well this morning. Thank you for that."

Doyle didn't say anything, he just smiled and went to his desk, removing his hat.

"Are you going to the gallery today, Arthur?" Marge asked from her desk.

"Yep, I need to start this case, and hopefully the police will be finished there," he replied. "I'm sure the death of the appraiser has something to do with the stolen object. But that's for me to figure out." Doyle looked at Oscar, "Guess who's on the case for the police?"

"Captain Cadeem?" Oscar replied.

"Don't even mention that name. No, it's Harry Lowe."

"Harry, well, good to hear that name. Do you need my help?"

"I don't know yet. After I talk to Walter Charles, I'll decide if I need help. Don't you have a cheating spouse case to go on?"

"I was hoping you'd need me," Oscar said with a grin.

"It still may happen, but don't give up your case."

"I'm always ready," he replied.

Doyle went through the mail, sorting out the bills from the junk mail. He finally stood and said, "I'm going over to the gallery now. Be back later." He put the hat back on and went out the back door.

He arrived at the gallery and saw that there were no police cars around the building. That was good, now he could start his investigation without interference. He went in and found Walter Charles in his office.

"Doyle, good to see you. I was so worried you wouldn't show up," Charles said.

"If I take on a case, I'm always on the job. Now we have to talk."

"Please sit, would you like some tea?"

"No, thank you, I'm not a tea or coffee drinker," Doyle replied.

"Well, excuse me if I have a cup. You can ask away anything you need to know."

"Okay, do you think that your appraiser was murdered because of the stolen statues? I just need your opinion, not a definite answer."

Charles was pouring hot water from a coffee maker into a cup, then he put in a tea bag. "I do think it is related. David was working on exposing the fakes from the originals. I believe the killer was trying to slow the progress of finding out which pieces were not the originals."

"Did he finish listing which ones were fake?"

"As a matter of fact, he did. All the statues in the gallery were examined and he had a list of nine artifacts that were missing. They were of great value, but the worst is they were all owned by the government of Egypt. I haven't talked to the representative of Egypt about the stolen articles yet. We have them on loan until the end of this month, when they have to go back."

Doyle did some quick figuring and said, "So, I have six days to find the stolen statues."

"Unfortunately, yes. Their director of antiquities will be cataloging the return of the statues and I'm certain he will see them as fakes. It could be a diplomatic disaster."

Doyle's Quest

"Okay, I'll need to talk to any employees who have come in contact with the missing articles. Does anyone else know the statues were stolen?"

"Only two others, my secretary, Mark Davis, and our security head, Len Ferigamo."

"You have security?"

"We do, a small team of six men and their boss, Len. They take shifts watching the gallery."

"What did Len have to say about the stolen goods?"

"He denied that his men were part of the thefts. He trusted all of them."

"Well, I trust no one. I'll need to talk to them first. Can you arrange it?"

"I'll have Len gather the men on duty now to talk." He picked up his phone and placed a call. He finished and said, "Len will gather his men and meet you in the conference room. I told him you have full authority to investigate. He is to cooperate with you."

"Thank you, I'll try to keep it all as simple as possible. Where's the conference room?"

Charles led Doyle out of the room and to another room that was large and open. There was a huge oval table with a dozen chairs around it. Doyle thanked Charles and he left Doyle alone. After a few minutes the door opened again and a man in a white shirt with patches signifying he was an officer of the security team came in. He was followed by three men in grey shirts with patches of the security company they worked for.

"I'm Len Ferigamo, head officer of the Arrow Security Company. You're Doyle?"

"I am, and thank you for gathering your men. I need to talk to all of them, especially the night guards."

"I just want to say that all my men are trustworthy and above board. None of them would stoop so low as to steal the articles in question."

"I'll be honest, I don't think they are the culprits who committed these crimes, but someone slipped in to steal the articles in question and murdered a man while your guards watched the building. I'm a former homicide detective of the Detroit PD, and to me, that raises a flag."

Ferigamo stood without speaking. Just giving Doyle a steely-eyed look.

*

Chapter 6

"Don't get your back up, Lieutenant, I'm sure you know your men and trust them. But, as I'm sure you must have figured, the thieves had to have had time to grab the statues and switch them for the fakes. There were nine missing, so they could have grabbed one a day to make it easier to do the switch. As for the murder, it shouldn't be hard for someone to come in and murder the man. You had men on at the time of the murder in the morning, correct?"

"Yes, my men guard the building twenty-four hours a day. There are many very valuable works of art on display here. Besides the statues, there are paintings by well-known artists that would fetch a hefty price on the black market. Also, my men have been questioned by the police about the time of the murder. They didn't say much if they had a clue."

"The police get very tight-lipped about their cases. I'm more interested in the thefts than the murder, I'll leave that up to the police. So, being as these articles that were stolen are well-known, who would want to steal them and not be able to show them, since they are stolen property?"

"There are many private collectors who would love to have these statues, just to have them in their private galleries in their homes. Never to be seen by the public. Such a waste."

"Being as you are in charge of the gallery security, you must have some experience in art works and their value?"

"I have worked at a number of galleries, in New York and here. I picked up a great deal of experience about the art world."

"What's your take on the thefts?"

"As you said, the statues could have been taken one at a time. Even my security system of cameras and anti-theft devices can be fooled by the right people. I don't think this was done by amateurs."

"You have cameras and anti-theft devices? I'd like to see them after we are done here." Doyle looked to the three men sitting at the table. He looked back at Ferigamo, "I'm sure you have questioned these men along with the police."

"I've interrogated them all and I find no problems that could be a reason for any of them to be involved in these thefts."

"How about financial problems? Any of them have money problems that would be solved by getting paid to look away."

"I've known these men for a couple of years and none of them are broke or in need of money. We pay well for our guards."

Doyle stood thinking, then said, "Okay, put your men back on duty. I'll reserve questioning for later, after I look over your security system."

Ferigamo smiled and called to his men to go back to work. They all shuffled out of the room leaving Doyle and Ferigamo.

"If you'll follow me I'll take you to our security office." He led Doyle out of the room and down a hallway. He approached a door marked 'Security' and he entered after passing a card through a scanner.

"Do all your men have door cards to get in?" Doyle asked.

"Yep, hard to do the job if you don't have access. There are a few more doors in the building that require these cards. I'll show you when we explore." Ferigamo took Doyle to another room off of the office. It had banks of monitors all showing various areas of the building.

"As you can see we can view any part of the building at any time," Ferigamo said.

Doyle moved closer to a young man sitting at the table in front of the wall of monitors. He leaned in to study one monitor where he saw a group of people standing in one room.

"We have groups of students from Wayne State and other schools come in to study the art works. Almost every day during the school term. In the summer it's dead in here. People go to the beach or up north, rather than view art."

"Can you bring up the camera where the stolen statues were?" Doyle asked.

"Larry, show camera five in the Egyptian exhibit," he said to the young man.

Doyle watched a large monitor come to life showing statues on pedestals roped off from the people viewing. "Those are the fakes from what I understand," Ferigamo said. "They managed to take all but one statue. I don't know how they could have taken even one. The pedestals are triggered to set off an alarm if a statue is lifted."

"How can the alarms be disabled?" Doyle asked.

"There are key switches in each room that turn off the alarms, the guards have the keys."

Doyle's Quest

"So back to the theory that a guard could be part of the thefts…"

Ferigamo didn't speak, then he looked at Doyle and said, "I don't like admitting to it, but I could be wrong. It would be the only explanation for how they could take the statues. I can't believe any of my men would be involved."

"Hey, I've known bad cops on the take when I was on the force. People will do anything for money." Doyle watched the people milling about the statues. The cameras covered the room quite well, as Larry, the tech, was scanning the room with a joystick, moving the camera. "Is Larry on all the time, or do you have another man on nights?"

"No, Larry works days and we have two other men who switch off to man the cameras at night."

"So, if one guard could turn off the pedestal alarms, the man watching the room would either have to be distracted or be paid off also."

"Geez, now you're saying two men could be involved? I don't think so," Ferigamo defended his men.

"Look at the situation. Pedestal alarms turned off so the thief could switch the statue and not be seen on camera. I presume you record all cameras?"

"It's all done digitally. No tapes, all on computer. I've already gone over the recordings and saw nothing."

"Look at the size of the statues. No human could carry a fake one in to switch without causing suspicion," Doyle said.

"I know, that bothered me too. Just one of the real statues is over sixteen inches high and weighs over fifty pounds of solid stone. It would take one big man to carry that off."

Doyle stood staring at the monitor, wondering about what Ferigamo said. How could they smuggle in a huge fake statue and switch it for an equally huge real statue and take it back out. Without being seen by a guard or on a camera.

"You reviewed all the video for the night shift?"

"Yep, we aren't open, so it was easy to skim through the videos. Nothing suspicious went on."

"I'd like a copy of your videos for the last week. I have a secretary who needs something to do."

"Larry, copy off the digital files on to a CD and give it to this man," he said to the tech.

"Give me about fifteen to twenty minutes," Larry said.

"While we wait, can you give me a tour of the Egyptian exhibit?" Doyle asked.

"Sure, follow me," Ferigamo said and led Doyle out of the room. They went down a series of halls and through a door that came out to the room with the statues in question. They moved to the middle of the room as a few people were walking around staring at the statues.

Doyle was looking for the camera and saw it in the corner of the room. It was scanning back and forth as he watched.

"Do they automatically scan or does Larry do that?" Doyle asked.

"Larry can control the cameras as needed but they are on an automatic scan," Ferigamo said.

"Do the hallways we just went through go to all the rooms?" Doyle asked.

"Yes, they're in the outer walls of the building so we can get to a room quickly."

"Could someone walk out of this room with a statue through the outer hallways?"

"The hallways all end up at the main office, then they would need a key card to get out."

"Well, I have to admit, your security is impressive."

"Thank you, Mr. Doyle."

"Unfortunately, it didn't stop the theft of nine statues."

"That's something I'll have to live with. It's going to be a thorn in my side."

"I hope I can clear your men and your system. This had to be committed by a professional crew. It's not a lone criminal."

"I believe that also. Anything I can do to help, let me know," Ferigamo offered.

Larry came out of the door and handed Ferigamo a disc in a case. Larry turned and went back through the door. Ferigamo handed the disc case to Doyle. "I hope your secretary will enjoy watching statues doing nothing."

"She's a very patient person. And she pays attention to details."

"You should keep her, then."

"I intend to." Doyle put the disc case in his jacket pocket and thanked Ferigamo. "I'll be in and out for the next few days, so expect me."

"I will. Charles said that I wasn't supposed to share the thefts with the police. Is that ethical?"

"Only if they don't ask you about it. It's best to keep this under wraps for the sake of the gallery, and keeping the Egyptian government from finding out."

Ferigamo smiled and said, "Have you ever seen those people, they are not fun guys."

"I know from my days in the FBI, I try to avoid them. You should too."

*

Chapter 7

Doyle studied the room layout, where the exits were and how the floor plan was laid out. "Which statue is still the real one?" he asked.

Ferigamo took him over to one statue on a pedestal with a sign saying it was in homage to Nefertiti. It was a bust of a woman's head wearing a very large cylindrical hat. Doyle leaned down to the sign and read the story printed.

"Neferneferuaten Nefertiti was the Great Royal Wife of the Egyptian Pharaoh Akhenaten. Nefertiti and her husband were known for a religious revolution, in which they worshiped one god only, Aten, or the sun disc. – Wikipedia."

Doyle looked at the other statues and said, "Interesting, this is the only female statue in the room. All the others are of men. Was our thief a misogynist and skipped the woman?"

"This particular exhibit was images of Egyptian royalty. It covered many different generations of Pharaohs and other big names in Egyptology. I guess Nefertiti was slipped in just on her name recognition," Ferigamo said.

"Sure, even I know who she was. Other than King Tut, I have no idea of who these other people were or their importance in the scheme of Egyptology."

"They all worshiped various deities. Ra, the sun god, was the most popular. The list of gods and deities is huge, even I couldn't memorize all of them. I guess it's simpler to have just one god and not be confused by so many."

Doyle's Quest

"Well, the Egyptians gave us so much in so many fields, I guess they weren't too concerned with memorizing all the gods. Do they still worship any of these gods today?"

"There are small fringe groups who still do, but most countries worship their own modern gods now. The gods of the past are mostly myth and legend now, but make good movies about mummies returning from the tombs. If you add the Greek, Roman, Aztec, Mayan and the Norse gods, this world has had its share of deities. It got crowded fast."

"Well, my concern is these Egyptian rulers who are missing. Where would the thieves go to sell the statues?" Doyle asked.

"I don't know of any antiquity dealers of stolen goods in the U.S., but there are a few outside the country, where the sale of such items isn't restricted. These statues would have to be smuggled out of the U.S. carefully. What with the security clamp downs for terrorist watches, they would have to take them out under the radar."

"I may have to call in a few favors from my FBI friends over this," Doyle said. "They would have an ear to such watches by Homeland Security. I'll have my secretary go over the video, just to get her take on it. She has a good eye for detail."

"Sometimes it's better to have an extra person take a look. I got really tired going over the videos, so my attentions waned a little."

"I'll be back, so expect me to drop in. Thank you for the tour, and I'll still need to talk with the employees who had access to this room," Doyle said.

"I'll make a list to have ready for you," Ferigamo replied.

"Thanks, I'll show myself out," Doyle said and left the exhibit.

Doyle sat in his car going over what he had seen. The only way to really find out how the statues were taken is to study the videos. He wasn't thinking that Ferigamo would lie about them, he even freely gave him the videos. Doyle hoped the videos were time stamped so he could see if there were any missing sections during the switches.

He started the car and drove back to the office. When he entered, Marge was on the phone. She waved to him and said she had to go. Then she hung up.

"Sister again?" Doyle asked.

"I'm sorry, she just won't take the hint."

Doyle's Quest

"You have to be firm and I'll get caller ID for the phones so you'll know when to ignore her."

Marge laughed and said, "Oscar is out following a woman who is suspected of cheating. There seems to be a lucrative business from cheating."

"Yes, and it's those small cases that keep us in the red. How's our finances doing?"

"We have enough to pay the rent, utilities and our income for the month so far. But no extras like pizzas."

"That's a shame. We'll have to buy store bought pizzas. Of course, we'll need a stove," Doyle said with a smile.

"Sorry, not in the budget," Marge replied.

"I have a task for you, so you don't get bored," he said and took the CD out of his pocket. He went to her computer and put it in the drive. After a couple of clicks he had the disc playing from the beginning.

"Okay, this is footage from the security camera for the times that the statues could have been stolen. I need you to carefully watch and see if you can spot any occurrence of theft of the goods. Anything out of the ordinary. Keep track of the date stamp, the thefts should have occurred in the night."

"Thank you, I was getting bored. My knitting is starting to get to me. I've made suits for both you and Oscar now that I got carried away knitting."

Doyle stood up and grinned. "I hope they're all in black. Colors don't look good on me. Now, watch the videos."

He went to his desk and sat. He needed to talk to a couple lowlife criminals he knew who may know where to get rid of the statues. He gathered his memories as to who he would need to talk to first. He thought of a couple hoods who dealt in fencing stolen goods, men that he had arrested in the past when he was a detective for DPD. He was still on good terms with them though. He made a couple of them his C.I.s to help ferret out criminals stealing property from houses and businesses.

He pulled his cell phone and went through his contacts until he found the first person he wanted to call. He hit the dial feature and the phone responded. He listened for a moment as the other end was ringing. Then he heard it connect, but he got a recording saying the person was not available, but leave a message if it's important. The recording ended and he heard the beep.

"Wilson, it's Doyle. Call me back, I need your help," he gave his office number and hung up. He looked over to Marge who was staring intently at the computer monitor, watching the room as the camera swept back and forth.

"Lots of statues. All Egyptian, I presume?" Marge said without breaking concentration.

"Yep, all Egyptian rulers and one queen," he replied.

"Only one queen? Seems rather chauvinistic of them."

"Nefertiti was the only statue that wasn't taken, also. I guess the criminals don't like female statues."

"Chauvinists," Marge said quietly.

Doyle held in a laugh and tried to call a couple more confidential informants on his list. One had disconnected phone service and the other gave a recording also. Was everyone out of contact? Doyle never left his phone far enough where he couldn't answer it. He sat thinking about how dependent people were to electronic devices. Remembering back to when he was younger, he had to seek out a public payphone to make a call on the road. That was a pain in the ass.

About twenty minutes later, he heard Marge say, "Interesting."

"What?"

"You need to come here to see this," she said as Doyle stood going to her. He leaned over her shoulder to watch the monitor.

Marge ran the video back a little and pointed to a man with a janitor's cart. "He comes in to clean but his cart is odd. Look how the mops and brooms are all sticking up on the side of the cart, blocking the view when the cart is in front of a statue. Also the cart is a big box and has no garbage bag hanging in the front. He doesn't have the cart blocking the view for very long, when he moves the cart off to the side of the room and continues to dust and sweep."

"Run that back to just before he put the cart in front of the statue," Doyle asked.

She played with the controls and ran it back. "Now watch the statue," Doyle said.

She stared and then said, "It turned a little. Before he put the cart in front, it was facing left, but after he moved the cart it was straight out. The statue moved."

"Someone moved it. Or I should say replaced it. There has to be someone in the cart with the fake to switch them quickly. One taken, then the guy moved the cart to draw suspicion away from the switch. Brilliant, Marge. Now we know how they were taken.

One a night. Run forward to see if that janitor did the same for different statues."

Marge pushed a few buttons and ran the video fast forward until they saw the man enter with the cart. He went to a different statue this time and the same procedure happened. He only had the cart there for a half a minute before he moved it away.

"I saw the cart shake a little on that one, someone moved inside it," Marge said.

"Those statues are very heavy, hard to move with that much weight. Also the janitor knows where the camera is and was able set the cart to block vision, even for a few minutes. Almost clever, but leave it to Marge the Magnificent to ferret out the culprit. Give yourself a bonus."

"If we could afford it," she said with a laugh.

*

Chapter 8

Doyle looked at his watch. It was still early enough to go back to the gallery to see who the janitor was. "Marge, can you copy off the video of the janitor onto a flashdrive?"

"I have a program that will let me edit it, yes," she replied

"You're a wonder. Do a couple segments of the crime so I can take it to the gallery to show the curator."

"I'm on it," Marge said and proceeded to work on copying the files.

A half hour later, Marge went over to Doyle's desk and handed him the flashdrive. "I copied the first three instances of the switch. It should be enough to prove your point."

Doyle stood, put on his hat and kissed Marge on the cheek. "That can be construed as sexual harassment in the workplace, but I won't tell," Marge said with a grin.

"I hope so. It probably won't be the last time I do that. Tell Oscar where I'm at," he said with a tap on his hat and he left.

Driving over, he was happy there was a small break in the case. He wondered if the janitor was even still working now that all the male statues were removed. The perp had to figure someone would catch on to the switches. They took all the statues in the Egyptian exhibit except Nefertiti, so maybe their job was done. There had to be two men, one to push the cart and pretend to clean and one to do the actual switch. But who shut off the pedestal alarms? The guards had the keys, but did they trust the janitor to have the keys also? Well, he would find out soon, he was pulling into the gallery parking.

He found Walter Charles in his office going through some papers. Charles looked up and smiled. "Mr. Doyle, have you found the missing statues yet?"

"A little too soon to say, but I found out how they made the switches." Doyle went to the man's computer and pointed, "May I use it?"

"Of course, what do you have?"

"I have the security videos of the Egyptian exhibit at night. I'll show you what we found." He plugged in the flashdrive and started up the program to view it.

"Now watch this part," he said as the janitor came in through the back door of the room. "Notice the cart, it's all wrong and it hides the statue momentarily while the switch is being made."

Charles leaned in and said, "The statue turned."

Doyle smiled that Marge said almost the same. "Yes, it was switched by someone in the cart. The mops and brooms hide the statue for a moment while they switch them. Then the janitor moves the cart away to the side of the room. My question is, does the janitor have the keys to turn off the pedestal alarms?"

"Not that I know of. The alarm keypads are out of sight of the camera as you can see. The man goes that way before the switch and then again before he leaves the room. He could be shutting off the alarms and then turning them back on."

"Who is this man?"

Charles stood and went to a file cabinet and searched through until he came to a file, pulling it, and bringing it back to his desk. "His name is Martin Rossi, he was hired through a janitorial agency about a month ago."

"About the time the switches started, according to the time stamp on the video," Doyle said.

"I see that. Do we need to bring in the police?"

"Let me talk to him first, then I'll call the police if needed. We don't want to put this out to the public yet. Wait until I recover the goods. Do you have his address?"

"I'm not sure, I'll look and write it down for you." As he was checking the file, a woman came in the room. Charles looked up and smiled. "Betty, what can I do for you?"

"Mr. Charles, I had a call for references for our janitor from another company's HR. What shall I tell them?" she said.

Now that was interesting, Doyle thought, and well timed, too.

"Is Rossi still working for us?" Charles asked.

"No sir, he quit two nights ago," she replied. "Actually, he didn't quit, he requested to be moved to a new location through his janitorial service. He's requested to work at the Masonic Temple and their HR wants to know if he's reliable."

Doyle looked to Charles and said. "Give him a glowing review. That way we will know where he's at. Now why would he want to work at the Masonic Temple?"

Charles said to the woman, "I'll send a reference shortly. Thank you Betty." The woman left the room.

"Was Rossi given a security check before he was hired here? This place has many valuable articles, you do check their backgrounds?"

"Of course. That's for Ferigamo to do. He contacts the janitorial service and gets Rossi's background from them."

"Easy for a janitorial service to place people in companies with lots of valuable possessions. Easy for the pickings. I'll have to check the company out. If you could give me the information on them, it may help."

"Of course, I'll give you that too." Charles wrote out and handed Doyle the addresses. He looked at the paper and said, "I may need to hold off until we see what Rossi is up to. Strange that he requested the Masonic Temple. Maybe it's where the statues will end up."

"I'm not aware that the Masonic Temple has or needs an Egyptian exhibit. I thought they were only interested in the Ark and the Grail and other such holy objects," Charles said.

"Masonic members are mysterious about their activities and I think Jesus had some involvement with ancient Pharaohs and rulers. Maybe there's a connection between the statues and the Grail." This was getting interesting, Doyle thought.

"True, Mr. Doyle. There may be a small connection. I hope you can figure this out, there might be something more to this than just a theft."

"The whole robbery was carefully planned and executed over two weeks. It was just an accident that you even discovered the thefts. I'm going to talk to the people at the temple and see what I have to do to get in and find out what Rossi is up to. I'll call if I find out anything."

"Thank you, Mr. Doyle. I appreciate it."

Doyle said his goodbyes and left.

Doyle had been in the Masonic Temple once before when he was chasing down the missing father a couple months back. The people there were friendly and helpful. He wondered how they would respond to his request for information about a contractor.

The ride wasn't far and he pulled into the parking lot in back. He was still amazed at the size of the building. More tall than wide but still big. He entered the main entrance, removed his hat and went to the front desk. It was a different man this time.

"Hi, I was wondering if I could talk to someone in your Human Resources Department," he asked.

"I'm sorry, we only hire through private contractors for building help," he replied.

"No, I'm not looking for work. I'm a private investigator and I need to speak to someone about an employee."

The man just stared for a moment then said, "Is there something wrong with one of our help?"

"That's what I'm trying to find out. Now, can you direct me to HR?"

He stood and went to a floor plan under glass on the counter, pointing out an office on the first floor. "You can go here to see Miss Moffit. She's in charge of hiring."

"Thank you very much," Doyle said as he went in the direction the map indicated. He went down the long hallway and came to a door marked 'Personnel' and entered. It was a large room with four desks arranged two by two. An attractive woman was at the only desk occupied, she smiled and asked, "May I help you?"

"I'm Art Doyle, private investigator. Are you Miss Moffit?" He held out his P.I. badge wallet to show her. She smiled and looked up to him.

Doyle's Quest

"What is it you need to know, Mr. Doyle? Please have a seat." She pointed to the chair in front of her desk. Doyle was attracted to her very blue eyes, almost like wolf eyes. He sat and relaxed.

"I'm on a case to track down some missing articles that may have something to do with a person who has requested employment in your building. He's with Darren Janitorial Services."

"I'm familiar with them, I presume this has something to do with Martin Rossi, since he's the only person that I have inquired about recently."

"Yes, he was a janitor at the Wittington Art Gallery and he requested to be transferred here. I need to know what he will be doing in the building."

"What is it you are investigating? He's not a criminal is he?"

"That's what I'm trying to determine. I'd like to keep an eye on him to see if he's up to something, and stop him before he possibly does something illegal." He was hoping to not admit the man was a thief.

"Did he do anything illegal at the Wittington?"

"It's an ongoing investigation and I need to keep track of him to find out if he is doing anything illegal."

"Well, Mr. Doyle, I couldn't possibly hire him if he's on the shady side."

Doyle leaned to her and smiled his best killer smile, "But you'd be helping me immensely."

She just sat staring, then laughed.

*

Chapter 9

"Mr. Doyle, if you're trying to look cute…okay, you are. But, I need some better answers before I can give you any of mine. What exactly is your plan regarding Rossi?"

"Okay, confession time, but I need to know you'll keep this to yourself," he waited, then she nodded her acceptance. He smiled again and said, "I'm trying find out what Rossi is up to. Yes, there were some shady activities at the Wittington, and I'm trying to sort that out. Rossi left the Wittington and requested to come here. I have to find out why, and only you can help. I need to watch him and see what he is doing."

"I actually made a request for two janitors. I'm sure you could be an undercover janitor working with Rossi," she said with a grin. "I watch crime shows on TV also."

"Works for me, but won't he be suspicious when I don't come in from his janitorial company?"

"Not really. I can say you are from a previous company and we decided that we didn't want to get rid of you. You were such a good janitor, that we kept you on." Now she gave him a cute smile, Doyle thought it was nice.

"Clever. You are devious, aren't you? I like that," he said with a grin.

"As I said, I do watch crime shows on TV. Sometimes I out guess the detectives, it's fun. But, you live this life don't you?"

"I used to be a homicide detective for the Detroit PD, but after shooting the mayor, I went into private practice," Doyle said modestly.

"So, you were the cop who shot the mayor? I heard about that. You're a celebrity," she said with a grin.

"I wouldn't go as far as that. I'm not happy it even happened."

"But, you did save his live from the gang that kidnapped him. That took a bit of heroism."

"Well, you had to be there," Doyle said. "Now, back to Rossi, I need to watch him to see what he's up to. I think your plan will work."

"I'll call the janitorial company and give him the green light to come in to work. You'll need to come in so we can show you the ropes. If you are an old hand at this, you need to know what to do."

"I'm on a tight schedule, so I need to move quickly. When can he start?"

"I can have him come in tomorrow morning and get him started by noon. When do you think you'll be able to start?"

"I have all day today. Do you have someone who can give me a crash course on the duties I would need to know to just get by?"

"Hold on, I'll call the one janitor left after the other two quit."

"Is he from the janitorial company that Rossi is with?"

She said, "No, he's an old hand that we kept on from the last company we used."

"So, Darren Janitorial is a new company you are using?"

"Yes, we had problems with the last one, so I contacted Darren and requested janitors from them. Bart, the remaining janitor, stayed on with us. He was a good worker even if his company was lousy."

Doyle was now wondering how reputable the new company was if they had criminals for employees. He thought about checking them out, too.

"Okay, I can start training anytime your man is ready," Doyle said. "By the way, what is your first name?"

"Jennifer, but since I am management, it would be inappropriate to call me by my first name during working hours," she replied.

"What about after work?" Doyle asked, flashing his cute smile again.

She hesitated, then said, "We can discuss that later." She picked up her phone and called for the janitor. She hung up and said, "He'll be here shortly."

"Thank you." He stood and said, "I have to make a call, excuse me." He pulled his cell phone and went out in the hallway. He speed dialed Marge.

"Marge, how's everything there?" he asked when she answered.

"Quiet. Oscar hasn't returned yet," Marge said. "There was one man who came in and asked about your services and I told him to come back in the morning. How are you doing?"

"I'm getting somewhere, though I'm not sure where. But, I'm progressing."

"Well, that's better than getting nowhere. Meet any women?"

"Marge!" Doyle exclaimed, "That's personal. But if you must know, I'm working on it. Now, go back to knitting, or watching videos."

"I think I'll bring in my portable television so I can watch soap operas or talk shows."

"You do that, I hate to think that you are bored. I'll talk later. I'm being paged." He hung up when Miss Moffit came out and waved to him. "Is he here?" Doyle asked.

"Yes, he came in through the service door. Come in and meet him."

Doyle's Quest

Doyle went in and saw the man. He looked to be in his seventies—grey hair, stubbly beard and well wrinkled.

"Bart, this is Art Doyle. It's a long story, he'll explain what he can, but you need to give him a quick rundown of what you do."

He looked a little shaky, but smiled. "New man, eh? About time, this building is too big for just me."

"Well, hate to disappoint you, but I'm temporary. I'll explain shortly," Doyle said.

"Take Mr. Doyle to your room and he'll go over what he needs," Moffit said.

"Fine, follow me," he said and went to a door on the side of the room. Doyle followed him out after giving Jennifer a wink and saying, "We'll talk later."

They went through a hallway to another door and entered. It was a fairly large janitor closet, with all the equipment to clean.

"So, what's the story?" the old man asked as he sat at a desk.

Doyle sat and went over what he had told Moffit about his case. Bart sat back listening, nodding every so often. Doyle wondered if he understood what he was saying.

"So, you're going undercover to find out if this guy is going to blow up the building or something?"

Doyle laughed, "Not quite that bad. I just want to find out why he wants to work here and what he's up to. Now, I think what I need to do is pretend that I'm a new guy also, and you can train both of us. That way, I can relate to Rossi, and maybe he'll loosen up enough to talk to me."

"Works for me. I used to be a cop in Eastpointe. I retired and took this job to supplement my social security. I understand what you're up to. Now, you want to give me a few more details so I know what to expect."

Doyle smiled and explained the theft of the statues in the Wittington. Bart listened intently and then said, "There's nothing here he could steal. There are some ceremonial objects the Masons use for their meetings, but they aren't worth much. I can't think of what he would want here."

That made Doyle wonder. Bart would know if there was anything that Rossi may want to snatch, so why was he wanting to work here? "Well, I hope to find out. If he doesn't talk, I may need to take him to a quiet place and beat it out of him."

Doyle's Quest

"You do that, and I'll stand watch for anyone coming," Bart grinned.

"I think we'll get along well, Bart. I'll go explain to Miss Moffit about the small change in plans."

"Miss Moffit is a hot one, eh?" Bart said, with a toothy grin.

"I was thinking that also, Bart. Good to have your opinion. I'll go talk to the hot one now." Doyle stood and said he'd find his way back and left Bart.

Doyle found the way back, it was simple. He went through the door to the HR office and over to Miss Moffit. "Small change of plans. Bart and I are going to pretend I'm a new employee so he will have to train both Rossi and me."

"Fine, I can say we hired you before we took on Darren Janitorial. I will let their other man work, but I'll have him come back next week to start. Don't want to tax Bart with too many people to work with. Rossi can start tomorrow." She gave Doyle a smile and said, "Now, about calling me by my first name…after work." She handed Doyle a slip of paper, it had a phone number written on it. "Don't lose it."

"I definitely won't. I need to go back to my office. I'll call this number after five." He turned to go then stopped, looking back to her, "This number doesn't go to a dry cleaning place does it?"

She laughed and said it didn't. Doyle went out of the office and back to his car. He made sure the slip of paper was safely in his pocket. Then he thought about Poppy. He didn't make any plans with her, so his evening was open. When it rains, it pours.

Doyle arrived back at the office and parked. Marge was standing looking out the front window at the traffic. She turned when she heard Doyle approach. "You got a call from the insurance lady. She said she approved your request to rebuild the cabin. She needs a contractor to talk to."

"I'll call my sheriff friend, Mike, back in Oxford and see who he knows."

Doyle went to his desk and dialed his friend. Mike answered and said, "I hope you're not calling to say you are sending crime my way again."

*

Chapter 10

Doyle laughed and said, "No, I just need an answer. Do you know of a good contractor to rebuild my cabin?"

"I do, if you don't mind that he's my brother-in-law," he replied.

"I don't care if the contractor was your wife, I just need to get the information to my insurance company to start rebuilding."

"You'll need some blueprints to start an estimate."

"Doesn't he have some standard ones he can work from?"

"Sure, I'll talk to him and maybe he can come down to show you a couple."

"Tell him to just pick a good one, bedroom, bath, separate kitchen and living room. You know what my cabin looked like, work with that."

"I'll do that. How's crime in the big city?"

"I'm on a case to find missing Egyptian statues, it's a real Indiana Jones adventure," Doyle said looking at his hat on the desk.

"Sounds intriguing. I'm glad you're not on a case that would involve shooting."

"Hey, Indy had a lot of gunplay. I'm not that far from being shot at."

"Well, remember to duck your head. I'll talk to my brother-in-law and have him call you."

"Thanks, Mike. Talk later." They disconnected the call and Doyle sat looking out the front window. Traffic was a bit heavy today. He remembered when his father would take him to Tiger Stadium around the corner from his office. Traffic would be a lot heavier than now.

The back door opened and in came Oscar. "I've had it with following cheating wives. I get all turned on watching them kiss and snuggle with the men they cheat with while I'm sitting in my car all alone. Do you have an extra woman you're not using at the moment?" he asked Doyle.

Doyle laughed and said, "Sorry, no. But if I find one I'll introduce you. Have a bad surveillance?"

"No, she was just all over the place before she finally met up with her paramour."

"Paramour?"

"It sounds better than cheating lover. I like to be up on what to call these people. Have you found out anything on your thefts?"

"I'm going to play janitor tomorrow to spy on my suspect. I hope to get him to talk about where he's hiding the statues or where he's selling them."

"You'd be a lousy janitor, I've seen your apartment."

"Hey, when I was with Val, she cleaned it up for me. I haven't messed it up badly since."

"Right, Val cleaned it. So where are you going to pretend to be a janitor?"

"The Masonic Temple."

"What's in there that needs your undercover work?"

"The thief who took the statues. He asked to be transferred to the Temple from the art gallery. I'm going to talk to him, janitor to janitor, about his activities."

Oscar shook his head and went to Marge. He handed her a manila envelope and said, "Here's my report on the cheating wife. If you're bored, could you type it up for me?"

"Sure, Oscar. It's something to do." She took the envelope and opened it on her desk. Oscar went back to Doyle.

"When do you start cleaning up?"

"Tomorrow morning. Why?"

"I don't have anything to do now, if you need help, I'm available."

Doyle sat thinking. "There's really nothing you can do. They only need one other janitor besides the suspect. Then again, maybe there is something you can do."

"Name it," Oscar said.

"Can you call around to your contacts and find out who deals in stolen antiquities, specifically Egyptian statues."

"I can do that. I've rousted a few fences in my career. I'll get right on it," Oscar said and went back to his desk.

Doyle's desk phone rang and he answered. "Art Doyle, may I help you?"

Doyle's Quest

"Mr. Doyle, this is Walter Charles, can you talk?" Charles asked.

"Sure, what's up?"

"I showed the video you brought to Lieutenant Ferigamo and he went to check the janitor's cart. It had a false box attached that was big enough for a man and a statue to hide. I had him take the cart apart so it couldn't be used again. Although, I think since Rossi left, there wouldn't be any use for it. We will hire a new janitor, but not from Darren Janitorial. Have you found out anything yet?"

"Still too early, but I'm going to talk to Rossi tomorrow and hopefully get him to confess, one way or another."

"You can beat on him if need be. Just get him to tell you where the statues are. Call me when you have something."

"I will." They finished and hung up. Doyle reached in his pocket and brought out the phone number of Jennifer Moffit from the Masonic Temple. He sat looking at the number and then turned when Oscar called to him.

"I got a contact who says he knows a guy who deals in Egyptian stuff. He's going to find his number and call me back. It's all on the down-low as it's illegal, so you'll have to be discreet. But, you are the epitome of discreet aren't you?" Oscar laughed.

"You have to stop listening in on my conversations, or I'll put the cubical walls back up." Doyle stood and put his hat on. "Indy has left the building," he said and told Marge he was leaving. She waved to him as she typed Oscar's report. "I have a hot date tonight, I'll call you if it gets hot and heavy," he said to Oscar and went out the back door.

In his car driving to his city apartment, he was thinking about both women he had met in the past few days. He liked Poppy, although she was changeable in a scary sort of way. He didn't know Jennifer too well, other than his brief meeting with her in the Temple. She was very attractive and had a good body as far as he could see. He never had to juggle more than one woman before, even when he turned down Amber because he was still with Val, he never cheated. But he didn't have a relationship with either of these new women. So he figured on playing the field until he saw where it was going. Besides, he knew what Poppy was like in bed, he'd have to compare with Jennifer. If it came to that. He laughed to himself. He was such a horn dog.

He arrived at his apartment and went in. It was now just after five and he pulled out the slip of paper again. He went to the phone on the wall by the kitchen and dialed Jennifer.

"Hello," came a soft and airy voice.

It threw him at first. So beautiful a voice. He hadn't noticed it earlier when he spoke to her at the Temple.

"Jennifer?" he asked.

"No, sorry, I'm Wendy. Jennifer is out. Can I help you?" The beautiful voice spoke again.

"Oh, is Jennifer coming back?"

"I doubt it, she's out with her boyfriend. She may not be back tonight."

Now Doyle was conflicted, she used him, and he felt like a fool. He was slightly pissed.

"Are you Doyle?" the voice said.

Now he was surprised and pissed. "Yes, I am. Jennifer told you about me."

"She did, and she apologized for leading you on. Told me to tell you if you called. She didn't think you would."

"Well, I did, and I'm not happy."

"I wouldn't be either. Would you like to meet me for a drink?"

"Are you leading me on also?"

"No, I don't play games with people like Jen does. She can be such a bitch sometimes."

"Where do you want to meet?" he asked her.

"There's a bar on Eight Mile by Hoover. The Coliseum, do you know it?"

"Of course I know it. I live about five miles from it. It's a strip club. You want to meet in a strip club?"

"Does that bother you?" her voice went softer. Doyle had to meet this woman.

"Me, no. I've been there. Are you going to show up, or will I be pissed at you too?"

"I'll be there. In thirty minutes."

"How will I know you?" Doyle asked.

"I'll be the only woman in a wheelchair," she said with a laugh and hung up.

Doyle just about dropped the phone. "What?" he said to no one in particular. He hung up the phone wondering if she was yanking his chain. Jennifer yanked him good, was this woman now trying his patience? He took a fast shower and dressed quickly. He drove the five miles to the club and parked.

He entered and paid his admission. He wasn't going to pay a hundred dollars for a private suite. He told the man that he didn't want a room, he was there to meet a woman in a wheelchair. "Have you seen her?" he asked.

"Sure, Wendy. She's in the back at her table." He pointed down an aisle and said to go that way.

Doyle walked through the club, it was busy with men at tables and dancers dancing or walking around. He had been there before and had a good time. If Wendy wasn't what he figured, there were many other women around.

He was coming through a group of people blocking the aisle and then saw her. She was in a wheelchair sitting at a table. There were four dancers standing around talking to her, so he couldn't see her face very well. He came up as a bouncer told the dancers to go back to work. The woman sat alone as he watched her. He still couldn't see her face.

"Are you Wendy?" he asked as he came up to her. She turned her head and he saw she was beautiful.

*

Chapter 11

"You must be Doyle. Jen was an idiot to let you get away," she said with that voice that gave Doyle chills.

"May I sit?" he asked.

"If you don't, I'll feel hurt."

Doyle looked at her chair and sat quickly. "Why is it you wanted to meet here? In a strip club."

She gave him a bright smile and said, "I used to work here. I was a dancer, but one night I fell off the stage and came down on the back of a chair right on my spine. It fractured and doctors did as much as they could do to fix it. So I ended up only partially crippled. Does this bother you?"

"No, honestly. I'm not bothered by it. Does being crippled make you less of a woman?"

"I hope not," she said.

Doyle's Quest

"Well, then you are still all woman, you just can't walk. You get around in your chair, so you are mobile. I'm sure nothing can hold you back."

"No, nothing. I'm pretty independent, and nothing stops me from doing what I want."

An attractive dancer came up to Doyle and asked if he wanted a lap dance. Doyle smiled and said, "No, thank you." She didn't look bothered by the turn down and went off.

"Did you refuse that lap dance because of me?"

Doyle didn't know what to say. He smiled and said, "I think it's rude to have a lap dance when I'm with a date."

"A date. Now I'm a date?"

"Does that bother you?"

"Well, no. I haven't had a date in a long while. Most men are bothered by my chair. Do you want a lap dance?"

Doyle looked around and said, "There's no one here I'd want a lap dance from."

"How about me?" she asked with a slight smile.

"Don't joke with me."

"I'm not. I still have some ability to move my body." She moved her wheelchair around next to Doyle and pushed up with her arms and slid over onto Doyle. He was amazed by the strength of her arms. She put those arms around his neck and started to move to the music. It was a slow song so she moved slowly.

"It's my legs that are useless. I still can move well enough to give you a thrill," she said with a grin.

"Yes, and you are doing that. Do I have to pay you for the dance?"

"You do and I'll never speak to you again." The song ended and she reached over to the chair and swung herself over. She wheeled around and parked at the table.

"You are amazing. I'm glad Jennifer stood me up. You can tell her that." She finished her drink, Doyle hadn't even ordered yet, so he stopped a waitress and asked for a beer and another drink for Wendy.

"Trying to get me drunk?" she asked.

"I suppose since you worked here, you could drink me under the table."

Doyle's Quest

"I did have to drink a lot, yes. I can hold my liquor. But you can try to get me drunk, I may even sleep with you."

Doyle tried not to show his surprise. "Well, that's an offer I'm not going to refuse. How many drinks will it take?"

"For you, not many. I've already decided I didn't need to get drunk."

The beer and drink came and Doyle paid. They sat staring at each other not saying a word as they drank.

"I think I'm sufficiently drunk, want to take me home?" she said as she downed her second drink.

"You know, we just met. You don't know anything about me," Doyle said.

"I know you are a private investigator, you almost killed the Mayor of Detroit, and you are very good looking. Even in your Indiana Jones hat."

"I didn't almost kill the mayor. He forgave me for shooting him." He pulled his hat off as he forgot he was wearing it. "The hat was my business partner's idea, and my secretary told me where to get it."

"Well, it suits you."

"How did you get here?"

"I have a friend who's a cabbie, he takes me where I need to go."

"So you'll need a ride home?"

"If he's not busy I can call him. Or, maybe you can take me home."

"I live about five miles from here and my apartment is on the first floor," he said with a grin.

"Shall we leave?" she asked, and started to wheel back from the table. She turned and went down the aisle to the front door and out. The bouncer at the door said goodnight to her. Doyle followed as quickly as he could.

"Let's see, you probably have a fast car," she said and pointed to the red Dodge Charger. "I'll bet that's the one."

"You are good. Yes, it's my car," he said as she rolled over to it and up to the passenger door.

"Are you going to help a lady get into your car?" she said.

He unlocked the door and she pulled up, sliding into the seat. "You're good at that," he said.

Doyle's Quest

"Lots of practice getting in and out of cabs." He took the chair back to his trunk, folded it, and put it in. He got in the driver's seat and drove out.

Fifteen minutes later, he had rolled her into his apartment and put her in the middle of the living room.

"So, I see you're a good housekeeper," she said.

"Don't let the place fool you. I had help," he said, remembering Val had cleaned it up for him. He just never got around to messing it up again. "Would you like a drink?"

"Are you still trying to get me drunk? You don't have to, you know."

"Well, I need a bracer, if you don't mind."

"Knock yourself out, just don't pass out," she said with a laugh.

Doyle sat on the couch as she rolled close and pulled herself onto the couch. "You really are good at that, aren't you?"

"I make a point of it," she snuggled in close and kissed his cheek. "When you finish your beer, you can carry me into the bedroom."

Doyle paused and then drank the bottle in one gulp. He set it on the end table and scooped Wendy up, carrying her down the hall.

Once again he woke around four, after having a bad dream about Egyptian statues riding in wheelchairs swinging mops, and coming after him.

He got up and went to the kitchen for a bottle of water. He heard something behind him and turned to see Wendy in her chair. "You're very stealthy aren't you?"

"I like to be sneaky." She wheeled back over to the couch and moved over on to it. Doyle came and sat next to her. "So, how'd you end up living with Jennifer?"

"She was also a dancer at the club. We got to be friends and decided to share an apartment."

"Jennifer was a dancer. Do her employers at the Masonic Temple know?"

"I don't think it ever came up. She never mentioned it. She was going to Wayne State for a degree in business and danced for the tips to pay her way through school. Me, I just did it because I liked the easy money and I liked dancing."

"Must be hard not to dance now?"

Doyle's Quest

"I got over it a while back. I visit the few friends I still have at the club every so often, to watch them dance. It's my therapy."

"Is there any type of operation that will let you walk again?"

"There is, but I don't have the money for it. I barely make ends meet with my lousy SSI check. I spent just about all my savings from dancing to pay for hospital bills. I'm still fighting with workman's comp to be paid back."

"It never ceases to amaze me how one little slip can cause so much damage. I've had cop friends who got shot in the wrong place and ended up in a chair."

"It has its advantages. I can get better treatment wherever I go. I don't play the pity card often, but it comes in handy."

Doyle looked at the clock on the wall and said, "I need to get you home, I have work to do. Jennifer is my new boss now. I wonder how that will go?"

"Her loss, you are very apt in bed. I give you five stars." She leaned over and kissed him on the lips. Her lips were very soft, Doyle thought, very nice.

She swung back to her chair and wheeled into the bed room to get her clothes. She was dressed before Doyle was. He still couldn't get over what she was capable of doing.

They were in his car and Wendy gave directions to her apartment. They arrived and Doyle got the chair from the trunk and she wheeled to the door. It was a nice townhouse on the first floor with a small ramp for the chair.

Wendy reached to the door knob and put her key in. She opened the door and went in. Doyle followed at her request. The apartment was spacious and accessible for Wendy. She rolled out to the living room just as Jennifer came out of a hallway. She saw Wendy before she saw Doyle.

"Where did you disappear to?" Jennifer asked, then she saw Doyle. "Oh, Mr. Doyle."

"It's after work, so you can call me Art," he said with a grin.

Jennifer looked to Doyle then to Wendy. "Oh, I see. I'm sorry I stood you up, please forgive me."

"I totally forgive you. If you hadn't stood me up I would never have met Wendy." He bent down and kissed Wendy on the lips, long and hard. He stood and said, "I have to go play janitor now, see you at work." He whispered in Wendy's ear that he would call her later, then he left.

Wendy smiled at Jennifer, "Well, you blew that one, thank you." She wheeled herself into her bedroom.

*

Chapter 12

Doyle had prepared for the day before he left his apartment, so he just had to stop by his office to check in, then go to the Masonic Temple. He parked in the back and went in.

Marge was at her desk and Oscar was out. "Where's Wonder Boy?" Doyle asked.

"He said something about seeing a fence and left. Why would he want to see a fence?" she replied.

"I asked him to see if he could locate someone who deals in stolen antiquities for my case. I guess he still has friends in the crime business." Doyle lifted the couple pieces of mail on his desk, skimmed them and then tossed them. All junk mail. "Good, no bills. I have to go to my other job, so I'll be gone most the day."

"Other job?" Marge asked.

"Oh, yeah, you don't know. I'm playing janitor to get information about my stolen statues. The suspect is going to work today at the Masonic Temple and I'm playing another new hire. It should be interesting to see if he will talk."

"You'll probably end up beating it out of him. Use a toilet plunger on him. That should get him to talk."

"Marge! You have a mean streak don't you?"

"After living with Max and listening to him talk about the crooks he caught, I have a sense of dislike for those people. Do what you have to do, within the law."

"As long as I don't get caught, I'll do it outside the law. Now, I have to go to work. Talk later. Oh, tell Oscar to call me if he finds out anything." Marge said she would, so Doyle left.

He arrived at the Masonic Temple and went into Jennifer's office. She looked up as he came in and blushed.

"Well, I certainly apologize for my behavior last night. I didn't think you'd actually call. Wendy was very glad you did though."

"I enjoyed Wendy's company. She quite a gal. Now, has Rossi checked in yet?"

"No, I told him to be in by nine-thirty, so he still has twenty minutes. You can go to see Bart and I'll say you came in earlier and I sent you to see our head janitor."

"That works for me. I need to set up some things with Bart, thanks." He stopped, turned and said, "Maybe sometime you and your boyfriend could double date with Wendy and me." He didn't wait for an answer, and left the office.

He grinned as he went down the hallway to Bart's room. He didn't mind getting stood up by Jennifer, it was all right now that he met Wendy. Then he thought about Poppy and wondered if he could juggle both of them.

He got to Bart's room and entered. "Well, Mr. P.I., how are you this morning" Bart asked.

"Please remember to not call me that until I get something out of Rossi. I need you to treat me as if I'm some new flunky starting in this job."

"I can do that. I've been a janitor for about eighteen years, it's not glamorous but it has to be done. I've hired and fired enough people to know how to deal with new people." He paused and then asked, "Have you ever done this kind of work before?"

"No, I haven't, this is all new to me. I'm not even very handy when it comes to cleaning my own apartment."

"Well, it's not very hard, just tedious. It's also repetitive, doing the same damn thing every night. I hate it when they have a concert or event in the auditorium. Those people can make a mess out of it."

"Don't you have extra help?"

"That's why they are hiring two new people. The last two were useless and didn't do a very good job. The Masons expect a clean building, so if it isn't done right, you're gone."

"You've survived this long, you must do your job right."

"I know how to spread blame when things go wrong," he said with a big grin. "Pays to have been here so long, I'm an institution in this place."

"I like that. Now we need to plan what I need to do today. Chances are Rossi won't be staying here very long. I'm just here to get info from him, so you'll be doing this again soon."

Doyle's Quest

"I've done it enough, so it's no big deal. So, tell me what you expect."

Doyle and Bart talked for about a half hour when they heard someone coming down the hallway. Jennifer Moffit and Rossi came to the door.

Moffit entered and introduced Rossi to Bart. Doyle smile and said, "Hi, I'm Lou Holmes, I'll be working with you." He didn't figure Rossi would know his real name, but may as will be cautious.

Jennifer said goodbye and left the room. Bart said to follow him. The three men left the room and went down the hallway to a larger room with cleaning equipment and he turned to them. "Rossi, have you ever used a floor scrubber before?"

The man stood looking lost. "No, I haven't. I didn't use one in my last location."

"Where was that?" Bart asked.

"The Wittington Art Gallery. They had a floor crew to do that. I was just hired to dust and mop rooms. They didn't use the scrubbers in most rooms so they wouldn't run into the pedestal displays."

"I understand that. These machine can do some damage. We use them on the hallways and the big auditorium. I'll have you and Lou start small, mopping and dusting like you did before."

Doyle and Rossi both nodded. Bart spent a short time explaining the room and its contents, then took them on a tour of the building. Doyle thought Oscar would love to see what he was seeing. Oscar had expressed his pleasure when he and Doyle came to the building while looking for the missing father. They hadn't seen much of the building then.

"Do they ever have secret ceremonies in here?" Rossi asked. "I mean like they show in movies, you know, human sacrifices and mystic incantations?"

Bart stopped and looked at Rossi, "Are you serious? I've never had to remove a body from this building or clean up blood. No, they don't do any of that hoo-doo you see in the movies. These guys are all businessmen, or average men, and some women who like to socialize and have a good time. Nothing evil or mysterious. I've been here eighteen years and never once saw a mystic ceremony or its aftermath."

Bart turned away and went into the auditorium. "This is the most work you'll do. They hold concerts here, both highbrow and rock and roll. So you can expect it to be a mess." He took them on a tour of the rooms off the big room and explained what they would be doing. Then he took them back to the janitorial closet. He gave them equipment to start cleaning the rooms in the auditorium and turned them loose.

Doyle's Quest

Doyle and Rossi took the cleaning carts out after they filled the mop buckets and gathered mops and brooms. They ambled down the hall to the auditorium as Doyle finally spoke.

"So, you cleaned the Wittington? I've been there a few times to see the artwork. Interesting place."

"Listen Holmes, I've worked a number of places and it's all the same. I only do this for the pay. Otherwise I don't care where I work, it's just another building."

"I understand that. Just wondering what you thought about all the valuable artwork. You, all alone in the building, with all that art worth millions. I wouldn't have thought twice about getting my hands on a few items," he said cautiously. "I've spent time in prison for theft. Something I couldn't help."

"And you got a job here having a record?" Rossi asked. "I thought they checked backgrounds"

"They do, but I'm on one of those rehabilitation programs. They're giving me a chance to make a decent living."

"So you still think about stealing. Not a very good rehab program."

"I can think, I just can't act on it. They have to evaluate my progress, to my P.O. and I have to submit to drug testing. It's a pain in the ass, but it keeps me out of the joint. I suppose you have a clean record?"

Rossi stopped pushing his cart and looked at Doyle, "Stop being so nosy. I'm not here to talk, just to work." He turned back to his cart and pushed it into the auditorium. Doyle was beginning to think this may require more action.

He followed Rossi into the room and stopped next to him just as his phone rang. He excused himself and went off to the side. Caller ID said it was Oscar. "What's up?"

"I got a lead on your missing statues. One of my C.I.'s told me there were feelers out for a big take of valuable Egyptian statues. It had to be under the utmost secrecy since the Egyptian government is involved in the ownership. I was told the statues were worth millions to private owners."

"Any word on who has the stash?"

"Nope, it's all being spread through the underground grapevine, so no names are revealed yet. But there's some scuttlebutt about some paramilitary anti-Egyptian forces at work here. This could be dangerous."

"Do they have a name?"

"My CI said they call themselves the Nile Liberators."

"Who the hell wants to liberate the Nile? It's a damn river."

"I don't name these idiots. I was told they aren't very friendly, so be careful."

"Thanks Oscar, I'll talk more later."

Doyle wondered how he would put this group into his conversation with Rossi.

*

Chapter 13

Doyle thought about his .38 in its ankle holster, in case Rossi was dangerous. He left his Sig and the shoulder holster out in the car since he couldn't wear his jacket. He looked back to Rossi who was taking a broom to the floor. He waited until Rossi came back by him.

"Hey, Rossi. Hold up a minute. I got a call from a friend and he heard that there was a big robbery at the art gallery you worked at. You don't know anything about it, do you?"

"That's a strange coincidence that you had a friend call about the place I worked at. What's that about?"

"Well, I came here earlier than you did and I was told you worked there. My friend called to see how I was doing and I mentioned you. He heard about the robbery and called me back to see if you knew anything about it."

"Is your friend a cop?"

"No, he's in the business of moving items that are not on the legal radar. He said that there were a number of statues taken from the gallery. He wanted to know where he could get his hands on said items."

"I thought your rehab was supposed to keep you away from crime. Why are you asking me if I know about it?"

"Well, you worked there and there are statues missing, just thought you might know something. My friend said he knows some people who would pay well for the items. Seems there are people who would want to add them to their collections. He mentioned that he heard some group called the Nile Liberators had the items." Doyle watched his face, but he didn't show any change in features.

Doyle's Quest

"Don't know anything about it." Rossi took his broom back to the floor and moved away. Doyle looked around to see who may be in the area, it was deserted. He reached down and pulled his .38 out of its hiding place. He walked up behind Rossi and grabbed his hair, pulling him back to the nearby wall. Doyle spun Rossi around and pushed him against the wall, putting his gun in Rossi's face.

"Okay, I'm not going to screw around, my sources say you had something to do with that robbery, now talk or I'll give you a bad limp." He lowered his gun to the man's legs, passing it across his crotch. "Or maybe I'll castrate you instead." He pushed the gun into the man's crotch hard. Rossi made a small cry.

"Stop moaning and talk," Doyle growled.

Rossi stood silently, so Doyle gave him another push in the crotch. "All right, damn you. Can we talk about this, one crook to another?"

"Talk."

"I did a job for very some nasty people. They needed to make money to fund their cause. They wanted the statues because they said it would be like a slap in the face to the Egyptian government, and by selling the statues, they'd have the funds to do what they planned."

"Planned, what do you mean by planned?"

"Has to do with buying a bomb, that's all I know." Rossi squirmed and Doyle held him tighter against the wall.

"I don't give a rat's ass about any bomb, or your friend's cause. I want the statues. Where are they?"

"I don't know," Rossi said. "They were taken as I got them out of the gallery. My friend Lonny helped to remove the statues and substitute fakes in their place. The Nile people got the fakes from somewhere and we took one each night and switched them."

"I know, I've seen the security videos from when you pulled your switch."

Rossi squinted his eyes, "What are you taking about?"

Doyle backed up still holding his gun on Rossi. "I'm a private investigator hired to find the statues and we saw the clever way you covered the statues with the janitor cart while they were taken. It's on video, so the cops may want to see them, and then they'll have you in their grip. Think about it."

Rossi didn't say anything, so Doyle continued, "We also have the murder of the Egyptian art appraiser to deal with. Right now, the police will assume you turned out his lights and are the number one suspect."

Rossi looked spooked after hearing about the murder. "Hey, I didn't have anything to do with that. I told you the Nile people were dangerous. I found out that Charles was having the statues examined and I mentioned it to the person who gave me the fakes. He said they'd take care of it. I didn't think they'd kill the guy."

Doyle put the gun down and yelled, "Bart, did you get all that?"

The older man came in and said he did. "All recorded on tape now. I knew the speaker system would be able to pick up what you two were saying."

"Good. I'll call my friend, Detective Lowe, and have him take Rossi away." He turned to Rossi again and said, "One other thing, why did you request to come here?"

"I was told to come here, to draw attention away from me for the heist."

"Does your company front the operations for the Nile people?"

"I don't know, but they tell Darren what to do, so maybe. That's how I got here."

Doyle looked at Bart and said, "I think I got enough for now. Sorry Bart, but you lost two employees."

"No problem, you both were lousy workers," he said with a grin. "I'll go tell Moffit to get me some good workers."

Doyle grabbed Rossi and pulled him out of the room. He took Rossi to the janitorial closet and zip cuffed him to a pipe in the wall. He pulled his phone and called Lowe.

Twenty minutes later, Lowe showed up with two uniformed officers. The men took Rossi away as Doyle explained the situation to Lowe.

"I had to turn him over to you. I didn't want you to arrest me for harboring a criminal. But, the theft of the statues has to remain off the radar. The Egyptians would be really upset to hear their prize possessions are gone. Give me a day or two to find them, then you can take the glory."

"I can do that. You caught and got Rossi to confess without your Indy hat. I'm impressed."

"You can stop that at any time now," Doyle grinned.

Lowe laughed and said, "Give me a call when you find the stolen goods. It will save me from having to find them." He left Doyle and Bart in the room.

"Well, Bart, it's been a pleasure working for you. Even if it was for so short of a time."

"Now, I got to start over. Moffit said she'd have two new guys in here this afternoon. So, I'll hardly miss you."

"I have to get back to my office and contact the curator of the gallery and explain this mess to him. Take care." Doyle went out of the room and back to see Jennifer Moffit.

She was at her desk when he came in the office. "So, I hear you caused quite a stir on your first and last day of work," she said.

"I'm sorry if I don't qualify for unemployment, but I do have another job, and I have to get back to it. Pleasure to have worked with you, however briefly. Maybe I'll see you again."

"You better, Wendy is expecting another date with you."

"I won't disappoint her," he said, then excused himself and left. He was back in his car and driving back to his office as he thought about what Rossi had said. He needed to find this Nile Liberation group, but where to start. He wondered if the FBI would

114

have these people on their radar. It was good that he spent almost ten years on the terrorist tactical force, so he still had friends in the bureau. He immediately thought of Kent Simmons, a feebie he had worked with. Last time he saw Kent was during the kidnapping of the mayor. He'd have to call him when he got to the office.

Doyle pulled in and parked, going to the back door and in to find Oscar at his desk. He went to him and asked, "Anything further on the Nile Liberators?"

Oscar looked up and said, "Nope, my CI said if he found out anything more, he'd call."

"Okay, let me know. I'm calling a friend who I worked with in the FBI," he said and went to his desk. He waved to Marge who was watching a small TV on her desk. Doyle laughed to himself and sat.

Marge came over and said, "Your lady insurance investigator called again about the contractor. Any word?"

"I asked Mike Twain to get in touch with one, he hasn't called back yet. I'll call him and get the ball rolling."

"I'll tell her you're working on it, if she calls back."

"Thanks, Marge," he said as she went back to her desk.

He lifted the phone on his desk and dialed his sheriff friend, Mike, in Oxford. A few rings later, Mike came on.

"Art, did my brother-in-law call you yet?" Mike asked.

"I've been out of the office, but my secretary didn't say I got a call. I need to get the info to my insurance company so they can start on it. Your brother-in-law has the job if he wants it."

"I'll try and reach him. If he doesn't move on it, I'll set my wife on him. He's afraid of his sister."

"Thanks, I have to call the FBI to find a militant group for a case I'm on. Have him call me soon."

They finished and Doyle looked through his contacts for the phone number of his friend Kent. He found it and dialed.

"Art, you're still alive?" Kent said when he answered.

*

Chapter 14

"Barely. I've just had about the greatest sex last night and the woman was handicapped. I'm not saying there's something wrong with being handicapped, but she was very good," Doyle answered.

"You have such a fascinating life, Art. You really should write a book about it. Giving tips on how to be Art Doyle, in and out of bed."

"Thank you, Kent, but I doubt it would sell. Now, I have a problem that you may be able to help with."

"Speak to me. I have nothing better to do at the moment. You know the FBI is slow right now," he said, sarcastically.

"I just need some intel on a militant group. Ever heard of a terrorist group called the Nile Liberators?"

"Talking about that nutcase group of men who want to pull down the Egyptian government? They were on our radar for a while, but they haven't shown any threats to our freedoms or done much else. Why?"

"I have a case finding some stolen statutes owned by the Egyptian government, and word has it the Nile nutcases are behind the thefts. It seems they want to sell the statues to buy a bomb. Does that raise them to a higher rank on your hit parade?"

"Who are they going to use the bomb on?"

"I don't know, it's not on my agenda, I just want the statues back."

"You never got any information about what they are up to?"

"My suspect in the robberies is clueless. He was hired to commit the thefts, but he knows little else. Unless you want to come down here and interrogate him? He's presently with the Detroit Police for stealing valuable antiquities and suspicion of murder. I'm still trying to find a fence who will try to push the goods and see if I can stop them before they go into a private collection, never to be seen again."

"We've investigated a number of antiquities thefts for various nations, and we've recovered a few of them. Do you need my help?"

"I may, can you be put on retainer for a later date?"

"I'll think about it. A case of scotch would be a nice retainer," Kent said with a laugh.

"I'll spring for a bottle of Jim Beam, that's more than you deserve," Doyle replied.

"Okay, JB Old Crow would be nice. I'll wait for you to call."

"Thanks, and if you can get any more info on the Nile people, I'd appreciate it."

"Will do, talk later," he said and hung up.

Doyle sat back and watched Marge watching her little TV and knitting. Oscar was on the phone, Doyle couldn't hear him. Not that he was going to eavesdrop, but Oscar was close enough to hear him, so he must be talking quietly. He stood and went to the front window and looked out to Michigan Avenue. Traffic was light, but fast moving.

"Are you bored, boss?" Marge asked him.

He turned to her and said, "No, just waiting for lightning to strike. I get this feeling when I'm on a case, I get a lucky hit and something comes to me that helps to solve the investigation. I'm hoping for that."

"Max used to say he got flashes of inspiration when he had to find a criminal. He had a good record of closing cases," she said wistfully, remembering her departed husband.

"They said he was good at his job. Too bad there aren't more cops like he was."

Oscar came up behind Doyle and coughed. Doyle looked back.

"Got something?" Doyle asked.

"Not exactly a lightning bolt, but a possible lead. One of my confidential informants said he heard there was a sale of statues going on down at Artie's Pawn."

"Artie's Pawn? Not exactly a high class place to sell valuable artifacts from history," Doyle said.

"Want to go check it out? I'm bored."

"Sure, let's go." He looked at Marge and said, "Hold down the fort. We'll be back."

She agreed and they went out the back door to Doyle's Charger.

On the way over, Oscar asked, "So, tell me about your big date last night."

"It was good. I got stood up, but met her roommate. She was very nice and good in the sack," Doyle replied.

"I overheard, not listening in, that she was handicapped?"

"Her legs don't work too well, but the rest of her worked just fine."

"Going to see her again?"

"I'm sure I will. Poppy hasn't made any advances so far, so I'll concentrate on Wendy for now."

"It must be a rough life having to juggle two women. Are you going back up north to see Amber?"

"Let's not get too complicated. I'll deal with what I have down here before adding her. She said I could visit when I was up at the cabin. I mean when the cabin is rebuilt."

"When is that going to happen?"

"As soon as Mike has his in-law call me about the price to rebuild. Then it will have to go through the insurance people before they pay out. I hope they have it finished before the snow sets in. October has been nice so far, but November is right behind."

"Going for a simple cabin like it was or something fancier?"

"I may change it up a bit, more modern. That cabin was over fifty years old. I've had it for twenty, so I had to put up with the way it was. I'll go for a few modern conveniences."

Doyle pulled up to the pawn shop and parked on the street in front. They got out and went in the front door. Both Doyle and Oscar were dressed causal so they didn't look like cops. They both still had jackets to cover their guns, but with the weather getting cold, it was appropriate. There was one man behind a counter, he looked like a slimeball to Doyle.

"Afternoon, Gentlemen. How may I help you? Looking for some nice jewelry?"

"No, we're more into Egyptian decorations. Kind of like statues. You wouldn't happen to have anything like that now, would you?" Doyle asked looking around the room. There were many articles for sale. Most items people pawned and lost because they couldn't pay to get their treasures back out.

"Gee, guys, I don't have anything like that, sorry," The sleazy man said.

Doyle leaned on the counter and spoke closely to the man. "Look friend, we heard you had some

Egyptian statues that you were pushing. We're interested, so don't screw with us."

The man looked nervous and was about to speak when another man came out from a back room. Oscar was behind Doyle and had his hand on his gun just in case. The man was well-dressed, over-weight and he smiled at Doyle as he came forward.

"Gentlemen, I couldn't help but overhear your request. Now why would the Detroit Police want statues?"

"We're not cops. So get that out of your head. I know a guy named Rossi who stole statues from the Wittington Gallery for a group of people called the Nile Liberators, and I want the statues."

The man changed expression, now looking serious. "The name eludes me. Nile what?"

"Liberators. As in, how we will liberate your ass from you if you don't tell us something."

"My, let's not get nasty now. I'd be glad to help you if I knew of any statues you speak of," he said calmly.

"As I said, we're not cops, so if we wanted to search your place, we wouldn't need a warrant and maybe if we did, we might mess your place up. So,

I'll be nice and ask again, do you have Egyptian statues?"

The man stood quietly for a short moment. "I may know something about statues, but we don't have anything like that here. If you'd like to look, feel free."

Either the man was calling Doyle's bluff or he didn't have the statues, as he said. "Okay, so what do you know?"

"First, I'd like to know who I'm dealing with," he said.

"The name's Doyle," he replied, "and the man behind me with his hand on his .38 is Mr. Drew."

"I thought you looked familiar," he said with a nasty grin. "You're the cop who shot the mayor."

"Wounded him, and I'm no longer a cop. Now, you want to tell me what you know about the statues?"

"What's your interest in them?"

"Let's say that there are people who want them back. I've been asked to recover them. And I'll do that at any cost. Do you want to find out how far I'll go?"

"Mr. Doyle, I don't have the statues. I have been approached to sell them, but I don't deal in such items, illegal I mean," the man said softly. Doyle had a good instinct for people and he felt the man was being truthful.

"Fine, you don't have them in your possession, but you do know who approached you to sell them. Feel like giving me a name?"

"If I did that, I would be betraying the trust of the person."

"I doubt this person is very trustworthy, I don't want to get impatient, I just need the name and I won't mention you."

The man went to the counter and picked up a notepad of paper and a pen. He wrote something on it and tore off the top sheet, folded it and handed it to Doyle.

"I hope this satisfies you, and concludes our business. Good day, sir." He turned and went through the opening to the back and disappeared around a corner.

Doyle stood up straight from the counter and turned to Oscar. He nodded and went to leave. In the car, Oscar asked, "What's it say?"

Doyle unfolded the paper and read aloud, "Irina Scoppolis, Egyptian Consulate."

＊

Chapter 15

"Egyptian Consulate? If the Wittington didn't want the Egyptians to know about the thefts, then why do the Egyptians have the statues to sell?" Oscar asked.

"Maybe this woman is a member of the Nile Liberators working undercover in the consulate. She knew that the Wittington had the statues and set up the thefts and is now trying to sell the things. Someone had to know the gallery had them to start. Plus Rossi said the Nile people gave him the fakes to switch with the originals. Someone in the Egyptian hierarchy would most likely have access to copies of the statues."

"Makes sense to me. So, she's working to bring down her leaders by funding the liberators."

"Egypt has been in turmoil lately with people trying to overthrow the government, so this would be a good time to strike. The money from the statues would help. Rossi said they were interested in getting a bomb. Maybe to blow up a government building? I may need to bring my FBI friend into this."

"You're not going to split the recovery fee with him, are you?"

"He can't accept remunerations for his investigations. Even if he could I'd only give him a small chunk. We need it more. Okay, back to the office to regroup." He started the car and drove out.

They came in the back door as Marge was gathering her things to go home. "Long day, Marge?" Doyle asked.

"It was good, with the TV and my knitting. You really need to find a way to bring in more clients."

"What, so they can sit around waiting for us to come back from investigating. Between us, Oscar and I can only handle two cases and the rest would have to wait. The one I'm on now will probably keep me busy for a couple more days, I hope. Oscar can handle the spouse chasing for now."

"Thank you for that," Oscar said as he went to his desk. "I knew I was good for something."

"Oscar you are an important cog in this wheel. Without you this firm would close up in a week."

Doyle's Quest

"Yes, I know. All these little surveillance jobs I do pay the bills. Besides, I don't have to work hard following cheating spouses. Mostly sitting around with a camera catching them cheating. It's them against us and we usually win."

"Very true, Oscar," Doyle said. "Now, Marge, go home and we'll see you in the morning."

"Yes, I'll see you then," she said and went to the back door and out.

Doyle watched her go, then said to Oscar, "That's one patient woman. I don't think we could have found another like her. A younger woman would be climbing the walls by now."

Doyle's cell phone rang out its *Jaws* theme and he looked at the caller ID. It said private. "Hello?"

"Art, it's Wendy," came the reply.

"How did you get my cell phone number?" he asked.

"While you were sleeping, I took your phone and checked it for the number. I wasn't sure if you'd call me back, so I wanted to be able to call you."

"Well, you are scary. What can I do for you?"

"What are you doing tonight?"

He paused, thinking, "I presume I'm seeing you?"

"I hope so. I'll dress especially for you. How about a nice dinner?"

"I can manage that. And afterwards?"

"I'll leave that to your imagination," she said with a laugh and hung up.

"Yes, scary," he said to himself as he disconnected the cell phone. He stood and put on his Indy hat, saying to Oscar, "I'm calling it a day. I have to get ready for a date.

"She have a friend?" Oscar asked.

"I'll ask her, but don't get your hopes up. Are you going home?"

"I'm going to work on my reports for the cheating spouses. Get them ready for the clients. I'll leave shortly."

"Okay, see you in the morning and we can go visit the Egyptian Consulate."

"Sounds like a winner," Oscar said and went back to his paperwork. Doyle went out the back door and to his car.

Doyle's Quest

At his apartment he relaxed, then got ready to go meet Wendy. He drove out to her place and knocked on the door. Jennifer answered.

"Well, back for more abuse?" she asked.

"I don't think Wendy is abusive. She's a delightful girl," he replied.

"Who's delightful?" Wendy asked as she rolled out from the hallway.

"As if you didn't hear. Are you ready to go?" Doyle said.

"Yep, where are we dining?" she asked.

"You'll see, it'll be a nice place."

He opened the door and followed her out to the car. She scooted over to the passenger seat and Doyle put her chair in the trunk. He drove out and over to a restaurant just down from his office, Ottava Via. Eighth Street was devoid of cars so he was able to park close to the sidewalk on the side of the building. He got the wheelchair out of the trunk and Wendy moved over to it.

"So, what is this place?" she asked.

"It's Italian, and they serve great Neapolitan pizza. Although I like Cloverleaf pizza, but we don't need carry-out tonight."

"We could have carry-out at my place," she said with a smile.

"Let's have a nice sit down dinner, carry-out another time," he replied.

He helped her into the building and to a table. They ordered and made small talk.

"So how is your case doing?" she asked.

"We're progressing slowly. These things don't just happen overnight, they take time."

"I figured you for a super-sleuth."

"Only when I have my super-sleuth costume on."

They talked a short while longer until the pizza came, then they ate in silence.

"So, what are you going to do about the operation to fix your legs?" Doyle asked after he finished off his slice of pizza.

"I have a lawsuit against the bar. Safety issues. The runway I fell off of had loose carpeting and I tripped on it. My lawyer says we have a chance of winning."

"Loss of livelihood and emotional distress, I presume? If it goes well, you should do all right."

"My lawyer thinks they might settle out of court, just to keep it out of the public record."

"Wise move, otherwise other dancers would be suing their keepers."

"That's about it. After they settle, I'll talk to my doctors about repairing the damage to my legs."

"Will you dance again?" Doyle asked.

"I doubt it. Besides I want to get a decent job and Jennifer said she could help me find one."

"Good for her. Now, I'm finished, shall I take you home?" he asked, raising one of his eyebrows.

"Only if you're going to visit," she said with a sly smile.

He went to pay the bill and took her out to the car. The ride was traveled in silence. Doyle was thinking more about the statues than the woman next to him. They arrived and Doyle helped her to her apartment.

She used her key to get in and Doyle asked, "Is Jennifer in tonight?"

"No, she's spending the night at her boyfriend's place. So we will be alone. There's beer in the fridge and I'll have a glass of wine, please."

Doyle went to get the drinks and prepared her wine. He came back out of the kitchen and she was gone. He looked down the hallway to her bedroom and went to it. She was already in bed, smiling.

"You certainly are quick," Doyle said.

"I don't waste time when it comes to bedtime."

He handed her the wine glass and set his beer on the bedside table. She downed the drink and slid down under the covers.

"I'll let my beer breathe awhile," he said, and undressed.

An hour later, Doyle had drifted off to sleep. He was worn out from Wendy and her ability to give him a run for his money. She did everything right.

He suddenly felt the bed move and peeked out to see Wendy in her chair going towards the door. The only light was from the bathroom next to the bedroom. He could see her shadow on the opposite hallway wall as she stopped her chair just in the doorway of the bathroom. He was suddenly shocked to see her shadow stand. She moved into the bathroom and Doyle got up quickly and dressed.

He went to the bedroom door were he could see the door to the bathroom. Just inside was her chair, empty. He knew the toilet was too far away for her to slide over and the shadow showed him she could stand and walk. He waited.

She came back to the chair and was shocked to see Doyle standing there. "Uh, I guess you caught me."

"What's the deal, are you scamming for the lawsuit?"

She just stood there looking sheepish. "I needed the money. The surgery for my spine was expensive and workman's comp was putting me off. My lawsuit was the only way I could get out of debt. Are you mad?"

"Disappointed," he said. "I think I'll call it a night. Good luck with your lawsuit, just don't make the mistake of standing too often. Lawyers have investigators who will find ways of catching you." He went to the door and out to his car. He should have stayed, but there was just something about fraud he didn't approve of. He might regret his decision in the morning, she was good in bed.

Back in his apartment, he laid in bed thinking about the day and Wendy. He would have to try and forget the fact she was pulling a scam for the lawsuit. It was her life and he wanted little to do with it now.

*

Chapter 16

Morning came quickly and Doyle hadn't slept well. He wasn't in a good mood as he got ready for the day. He wasn't sure if he was mad at himself for leaving Wendy vulnerable. He really didn't give her much of a chance to explain herself. He sort of felt like a heel for leaving her alone like that. Maybe he'd call her later and have a talk.

He arrived at his office and went in the back door. Oscar wasn't in, but Marge was at her desk with the TV and her knitting. She smiled and waved as he came in. He put his hat on his desk and went to her.

"Marge, don't you get bored here?" he asked.

"Oh, goodness no. It's here or be totally bored at home. I'd rather be here doing the same things I'd do at home. I'm fine, don't worry. You have more important things to worry about."

"Thank you, Marge. I'm glad you're working for us," he said and went back to his desk to check the mail.

He heard the front door open and looked up to see a woman enter. He suddenly realized it was Wendy. She had those crutches that attach to the arms and moved into the room on them. He stood and signaled Marge that he had it.

He stopped in front of her, as she said quickly, "I'm sorry about this morning and not confiding in you. Yes, I was using the chair for the lawsuit, but I do have problems with my legs. I do need these crutches to walk. I can go short distances without them but I'm probably going to have to use them the rest of my life. May I sit?"

Doyle led her to the client chair and let her sit. He sat and said, "I'm sorry for leaving so abruptly, without giving you a chance to talk."

"I don't blame you. I was wrong to use the chair, but I'm broke and it was the only way to get out of the debt I built up. You and Jennifer are the only people who know I can sort of walk. But I'll never dance again. I was making good money at the club dancing. It's hard to be broke after you've made good money. I called my lawyer this morning and explained. He said since I was still actually crippled, I could go on with the lawsuit, but he advised against using the chair."

"Wise decision, you would have lost the suit and probably been charged with fraud. I'm glad to see you can walk, as well as you can. Let's put this morning behind us and start over."

"I'd like that. You are a good man and they are hard to find. I endured all the lecherous creeps at the bar, it's been refreshing to have someone I can appreciate."

"How did you get here?" Doyle asked.

"Jennifer dropped me off on her way to work. I can take a taxi home."

"No, I'll drive you back after my partner gets here. We have some investigating to do today. When my case is finished I'll take you out for dinner again, and this time you can walk into the restaurant."

"That will be nice. Thank you for understanding."

Doyle looked back as he heard the back door open, it was Oscar. He called to him to come over.

"Oscar, this is Wendy. Wendy this is my partner, Oscar."

"Nice to meet you, Wendy," Oscar said holding his hand out. She took it and smiled. "Are you ready to go checkout the consulate?" he asked of Doyle.

"Yes, but we need to drive Wendy back to her place, then we will." He looked at her and said, "Shall we go?"

She stood and he helped her. They went out the back door, going slow so Wendy could keep up. She did fairly well on the crutches, Doyle thought. They arrived at her apartment and Doyle helped her to the door.

"Look, I'd like to see you again, if you want," she asked him after she unlocked the door.

"I'd like that, we'll take it slow this time," he replied.

She leaned to him and gave him a kiss, "Thank you. Call me." She went in and Doyle went back to his car.

"Is she the one who was in a wheelchair?" Oscar asked, as they pulled away.

"Yes, but she can get around without it. Now we have to put our heads into finding out what is going on with the statues. Time is running out for when the Egyptian's will take back their statues from the gallery. They'll find out they are fakes and that could be bad."

"Think they will go to war with the United States over it?" Oscar said with a smirk.

"Hardly, but the Wittington could be liable for the cost of the statues. That could ruin them."

"Did you look up where the consulate is?" Oscar asked.

"Yep, there are a number of Egyptian citizens who live here, so they put the consulate over in Dearborn."

"I thought that area was mostly Arab types?"

"You mean Muslims, yes. But the Egyptians live there also. The consulate serves their community. It's actually two consulates next to each other. Dearborn has the largest, and still growing, Muslim population in the United States and the second largest Arab population outside of the Middle East. Hopefully we won't have any problems."

"All we need to do is talk to this woman about her activities. Think we should call ahead and make an appointment, and not ambush her?" Oscar asked.

"I already did, before you came in. I didn't say what it was about, so she'll still be ambushed."

Doyle's Quest

"What exactly is her job there?"

"She's a promotional director for community activities. She handles events for the community, like fairs, gatherings and art displays. I said I wanted to talk about displays for an event of Egyptian art."

"Close to the fact, I'd say. Think she may clam up if we mention the Nile people?"

"If she does, it will tell us something. I don't think they would have the statues in the consulate, they must be stored elsewhere. I doubt she'll tell us, so we need to be clever."

"Well, that leaves you out, you're about as clever as a bull in a China shop." Oscar said.

Doyle just laughed and drove on.

They arrived at the building and parked. It wasn't so much like a consulate in some countries. They had no guards to prevent you from entering. It was more of a community cultural center. They found a woman at a desk by the door and Doyle asked for Irina Scoppolis. The woman directed them to her office.

At the door Oscar asked, "Are we going to get right to the point or beat around the bush?"

"We'll take it slow and see what we can get. I'm going with plan B." Doyle said with a grin, and opened the door. It was a nice office, with decorations from the Middle East. Doyle saw no statues.

"Hello, gentlemen. You must be Mr. Holmes?" A woman seated at a desk asked.

They moved forward and Doyle said he was and introduced Oscar as Drew Watson. She asked them to sit, they did.

"Now, what may I do for you?" she asked.

"We want to know how we can purchase the statues that the Wittington Gallery has on display. Are they for sale?"

She looked surprised. "No, Mr. Holmes. Those statues are antiquities and very valuable. Why would you want to buy them?"

"We represent a very wealthy man who made a fortune with the internet. He's of Egyptian descent and has his home decorated in antiquities very much like your statues. He wants to remain anonymous, which is why we are making inquiries on his behalf. He saw the display at the Wittington and wanted to find out if he could purchase them. He's a billionaire and money isn't an issue."

Doyle's Quest

Doyle could see the gleam in her eyes when he mentioned the money aspect. She sat back in her chair and was silent. They gave her time to think.

"Mr. Holmes, if we were to sell the statues at the Wittington, you could just take them from the gallery when our display agreement runs out later in the week."

"Well, now there's the problem. We had our appraiser examine the statues and he reports that they are fakes. Our employer wants the real ones. Do you have them?"

Now she looked distressed. "You had them examined? By whom?"

"A young man named David Mostafi." Doyle didn't mention he was murdered, he watched for her reaction, she gave none.

"I don't know who that is, but I'm sure your employer wouldn't want to purchase fakes. We sometimes loan out statues to smaller galleries like the Wittington, but we substitute replicas instead of the real articles. That way our valuable artifacts are safe from harm or theft."

"So you knew the statues at the Wittington were replicas?"

"Yes, as I said, it's safer that way and no one knows the difference. Unless they have an examination done as you did. Now I'm sure the Wittington will be offended by our ruse."

"We haven't informed the Wittington, so your secret is safe. Now, as to the real statues, are they for sale?"

"Mr. Holmes, I can speak for our government, I'm sure they don't want our precious past to be sold out. However, maybe something can be arranged if you and your employer are very discreet."

"I will say that our employer has a number of items in his collection that are from unsavory sources. Not saying you're unsavory, but he's not above buying stolen items."

"Well then, Mr. Holmes, maybe something can be arranged." She sat back and gave them an evil smile.

*

Chapter 17

"I'm listening," Doyle said.

The woman sat back, quietly thinking. Doyle was hoping she wasn't going to punk out on the deal now that she was loosening up.

"Mr. Holmes, what assurances do I have that you aren't trying to entrap me? My government doesn't take kindly to giving away their treasures. I'm not saying I can sell the statues, they're not mine to sell."

Doyle now figured she may have gotten cold feet or suspected something. "Well, then I'll leave you a number you can call me at if you decide what you want to do. I don't want you to think we are making trouble for you. We're not the police or representatives of your government, or any other official agency. We are only interested in the statues, not where they come from or who has possession of them."

Doyle took out his notepad and wrote a number on it. Doyle had purchased a burner phone a while back in case he needed a number for people to call, and it couldn't be traced back to him. He gave her that number, and stood. "This is the number I can be reached at. I hope to hear from you or someone.

Thank you for your time." He signaled to Oscar and they left.

Outside at the car Oscar asked, "Think we'll get a call?"

"Of course. She took the bait, but was being careful. We approached her, she didn't come to us. She doesn't know us and will probably have someone from the Nile people call to verify we are honest crooks and really interested in buying the statues. Now, we need to get back to the office to where I have my safe phone."

He drove away from the building and arrived back at their office. Marge was at her desk on the phone as Doyle and Oscar came in the back door. She waved to Doyle and pointed to the phone. Covering the mouthpiece she whispered, "It's the man from the gallery."

Doyle said, "I'll take it. Tell him to hold on."

Marge said, "Mr. Doyle has just arrived, please hold." Doyle hit the button to answer and Marge hung up.

"Mr. Charles, how are you today," Doyle said, hitting the speaker button so Oscar could hear.

Doyle's Quest

"I'm feeling tense, Mr. Doyle. It's getting closer to the deadline for the Egyptians to reclaim their objects. What have you found so far?"

Doyle explained about confronting Rossi at the Masonic Temple and about finding the pawn shop where they got a lead on the statues.

"The woman said she knew that the original statues you were given were replicas, but I don't believe her. Why go through the trouble to steal replicas? They had to be the real items and now they are in possession of the people that we are waiting on to call us. That's all I can say for now, but we can implicate the woman if the Egyptians find out the statues you have are fake. I'll explain more when we get word. Thanks for calling and don't worry." They finished the call and hung up.

"How will you implicate the woman? It's your word against her word," Oscar said.

Doyle grinned and reached into his coat pocket taking out a small device. "This is a digital recorder, I recorded the whole conversation. That's how I'll implicate her. She didn't come out and admit to having the statues, but she said a few lies about them being in the gallery. It'll be enough to cast doubt on her."

"You sometimes amaze me. You could have told me you were recording the conversation."

"I didn't think it was necessary at the time, I'm telling you now. So, we wait for a call." He reached into the bottom drawer of his desk and brought out the extra phone. He plugged the charger in since he hadn't been charging it lately. An oversight he would have to take care of more often.

Oscar went to his desk and sat staring at the paperwork piled up in front of him. "I need to hire a personal assistant to take care of my reports."

Marge heard him and said, "You have me to take care of that stuff, Oscar. I'll be glad to help."

Oscar grinned and picked up the pile, taking it to Marge. "Thank you, Marge. I just need all the notations I made typed into a clean report for the client. I'm not very good at typing."

"What did you do when you were a police detective and had to type up your daily reports?" Doyle asked.

"I usually had one of the junior grade detectives do it. I told them it was good training for when they achieved rank."

"Passing the work off, I would expect you to do that," Doyle said just as the phone on his desk buzzed and jumped around. Doyle figured it had to be about the statues, since no one else had the number.

Doyle's Quest

He picked up the phone and said hello. He flipped it to speaker as soon as Oscar came over.

"Are you the man who inquired about some articles that you wanted to buy for another person?" a male voice said, being cautious.

"I am, and who am I talking to?"

"That's neither here nor there, not important. I was told you represent a wealthy client who is interested in the statues on display in the Wittington?"

"We know those statues are fakes, my client wants the originals only. He is willing to pay whatever it takes."

"Let's say I know where the originals are and I may be able to strike a deal on them. How much is your client willing to go?"

"Why don't you make an offer, and I'll tell you if he's willing to go there."

The man paused and it sounded like he was whispering to someone else. Doyle and Oscar waited until the man finally said, "We are willing to part with the statues for three million dollars."

"Three million? That's pretty steep, but I think my client would be willing go for that. But only if the statues are the originals. I would have to bring in my appraiser to verify you have the real deal."

There was another pause, and then the man said, "You can see one statue, that's all. The rest will remain hidden until you come up with payment. Where do you want to meet?"

"Do you know where the former Tiger Stadium is at?" Doyle asked.

"I do."

"Next to that is a parking lot off Cherry Street and Cochrane Street. We can meet there, it's open and safe. What time can you be there?"

They were silent again. "We can be there at three this afternoon. Can you have your appraiser there?"

"We'll be there, just have the statue," Doyle said and hung up.

"Where are we going to get an appraiser?" Oscar asked.

"Doesn't matter, they'll have a real statue, or they'll queer the deal if they bring a fake and we have an appraiser with us. Now we have to find someone to play an appraiser." He thought for a moment then said, "I have a great idea." He took out his cell phone and speed dialed. After a minute he said, "Harry Lowe, please, Art Doyle calling."

Oscar grinned, "Do we have to split the recovery fee with Harry?" he said.

"Don't be silly, Harry can make the final bust and we get to return the statues."

"Won't they take the statues into evidence?"

"That's true, I'll have to get Harry to make a deal," Doyle said as Lowe came on the phone.

"What do you need, Indy?" Lowe said with a laugh.

"I'm not wearing my hat right now, just need a favor."

"Is this about the missing statues?"

"Yeah, we have a lead and need someone to pretend to be an appraiser to verify the statue we are going to see is real."

"Doyle, you know I know nothing about art thingies. But, I do know someone who can help you. He works in our forensics, he's Arabic and he likes that stuff. I'll have him call you."

"Make it quick, we have to go see the suspects in two hours."

"I'll call now and have him get with you. Later," he said and hung up.

"Well, this may work out well. He sounds like he could pass for an appraiser." Doyle said sitting back.

About forty minutes later, Mahmoud Safar arrived at Doyle's office and introduced himself. "Welcome Mahmoud, have a seat while I explain the whole mess for you," Doyle said.

They sat talking and explaining the situation. Mahmoud sat listening, nodding his head. "So, you'll have me to play the person who will examine the statue to say it is real. I do know about these things, having trained in archeological forensics in Cairo. Are these people dangerous?"

"We don't exactly know, but we'll be armed in case. I'm not taking any chances. We need to get them to talk about where the rest of the statues are, which I'm sure they won't want to say. You just need to look at the statue and do something to look like you know what you are doing and say the statue is real."

The man reached down and picked up the case he brought with him and set it on the desk. He opened it and showed Doyle and Oscar the contents.

"These are my tools I used in Cairo to test artifacts, so it will be a real test of the object I will make."

Doyle was impressed. "I'll have to thank Lowe for you. It may cost me a good bottle of whisky, but it will be worth it. Oh, and one for you."

Doyle stood as Mahmoud closed up his case. "Shall we go and set up the meeting place? I also have something else you will need to do."

*

Chapter 18

Doyle went to the boxes, still packed, at the back of the large office. He opened one and took out a small box, taking it back to Mahmoud. He opened the box and took out a tiny device and said, "This is a tracker. I don't think the people we're meeting will think that we'll bring one. Do you think you can attach this to the statue, so we can follow it back to the source?"

"If the statue has some place to hide it, yes," he replied.

"Good, here's some putty to use to stick it to the statue. The place we are meeting is around the corner by the old Tiger stadium property. The stadium is gone, but the parking lots are still there. Oscar and I will keep the men busy while you examine the statue," Doyle said.

"Hopefully, it will all go to your plan," Oscar said. "I presume this is your plan B?"

"Of course, it's always been good to us in the past. All right, let's go," Doyle said and they went to the back door and out to Doyle's car.

The drive was very short, just crossing Trumbull Road and around the property of the former stadium. They were early, no one else was there. So they waited, making small talk about Mahmoud's experience with Egyptian artifacts. About ten minutes later, a SUV pulled in and drove over to them.

"Mahmoud, wait in the car until I signal you. I want to be sure they aren't dangerous." Doyle and Oscar exited the car and went around to the front of the vehicle.

The SUV had tinted windows so it was hard to tell who was inside. The doors finally opened and out came three ethnic looking men of Middle Eastern descent. Two of them went to Doyle and Oscar.

"You are Holmes?" one man asked.

Doyle's Quest

"I am," Doyle replied, "and you are?"

"No one you need to know. We have the statue, do you have your appraiser?" he replied.

"We do. Bring the statue to the hood of my car so he can examine it."

The man signaled to the third man standing by the SUV and he opened a door. The large man reached in and brought a heavy cloth covered object out. He walked to Doyle's car and set it on the hood.

"Don't scratch the car, please. It's still almost new," Doyle said, and then signaled for Mahmoud. He got out of the car with his case and came forward.

"This is our appraiser, Mr. Safar, he'll examine the statue." Doyle signaled to Mahmoud to go ahead with his examination.

He approached the covered object and pulled the cloth down. He stood staring at the statue for a few seconds then looked at Doyle "This is the bust of Ramesses the second, also referred to as Ramesses the Great. He was the third Egyptian pharaoh and reigned in 1279 BC of the Nineteenth dynasty. He is often regarded as the greatest, most celebrated, and most powerful pharaoh of the Egyptian Empire. This bust is a recreation of a larger statue. They were often made for display in the temples. If it is ancient, I'll know in a few moments." He brought his case up and placed it carefully on the hood of the car and opened it.

While Mahmoud was fussing with his tools, Doyle stepped over to the men, diverting their attention from Mahmoud. "So, I talked to my client and he said that three million was a little steep. He's offering two million and if that's not negotiable, then he may not be interested in purchasing the goods."

The man who seemed to be the leader looked confused. "I was told that three million was on the table."

"It may have been on the table, but it was not agreed on yet. After my friend checks the validity of the bust, we'll talk money."

While they were talking, Mahmoud found a small nook in the statue that would hide the tracker. He pushed the device in with the putty, and it stayed in place. He proceeded to make his appraisal of the statue.

The leader said, "I have people to answer to for the sale of the statues. I can't negotiate terms. They set the price, so it will be what they want."

"Well, then call your people and tell them the new terms. Two million cash, no questions, in exchange for the statues," Doyle said.

Doyle's Quest

The man looked frustrated, Doyle assumed he was not such a hardcore criminal and was just speaking for his people. The man moved away from Doyle and pulled his phone, placing a call. Doyle went to Mahmoud and asked how it was going.

"The bust is genuine, and I've found a place to put your device," he said quietly. "This is worth about one-hundred thousand dollars on the open market. It should never be on the open market, this is part of Egypt's heritage."

"A hundred K? They have nine statues all together, so that would figure to be about a million easy. Depending on the worth of the other statues."

"Most of the busts and statues in the exhibit were about the same worth. I checked the internet on my phone for the Wittington's Egyptian display. The ones they had were all lesser antiquities. Recreations of larger statues to be used by the Pharaohs to bolster their egos. As you said, about a million dollars in value for all."

Doyle was thinking about the recovery fees. He glanced back at the man on the phone who looked very animated. Doyle couldn't hear what he was saying, but he didn't look happy. Doyle went to him.

"Excuse me," he said, and as the man looked back to him, Doyle continued. "My appraiser said the bust is genuine, but it's worth only around one hundred thousand dollars. So, with the other eight my client wants, that would be less than one million dollars total. I'd have to talk to my client to see how he wants to handle this now."

The man spoke into the phone in a language Doyle couldn't understand. He still didn't look happy. He hung up his phone after a short conversation, looking to the statue often.

"My people say they will take the offer of two million. The statues may be worth one million, but the extra cost to get the objects to you will cover the increase in danger for us. We are taking a great risk even putting the objects up for sale. If the leaders of the government find their valuables are being pillaged, our lives would be in jeopardy. So, talk to your employer and see what he says."

Doyle smiled and said, "Take your bust and call me later today. My client is a busy man and I may have trouble reaching him." He turned and went back to Mahmoud telling him to pack it in. The big man took the statue from Doyle's car and went back to the SUV. Doyle waved to Oscar and Mahmoud to get into the car.

In the car, Oscar asked, "So what now?"

"We need to go back to the office and get on the computer to find out where the tracker leads us,"

Doyle said, then directed his attention to Mahmoud. "You did turn on the tracker?"

"Turn on the tracker?" Mahmoud said looking surprised. "I wasn't told it needed to be turned on."

Doyle looked at Oscar and uttered, "Crap, a detail I didn't think about." Doyle looked back at the SUV, it had already pulled out of the parking lot. Too late to follow. "Well, they'll call and we'll have to regroup on our plan."

"Sorry guys, if I had known I would have turned it on," Mahmoud said.

"Not your fault, I should have thought about it. I'm getting forgetful. Well, let's go relax until we hear from them." Doyle started the car and drove across Trumbull to the office. They went in and Marge greeted them.

"So, how did it go?" she asked.

"Don't ask," Doyle said quietly.

"Art forgot to tell Mahmoud to turn on the tracker," Oscar said with a grin.

"Oh, dear. So you can't follow them?" Marge asked.

"Nope, we have to figure out a new plan," Doyle said as Oscar and Mahmoud stood watching him.

"Well, if they agree to whatever you plan to offer them, they'd have to let us see the merchandise. We know where the stuff is then," Oscar said.

"Very true, Oscar. Now I have to figure how we will give them any money, least of all two million dollars. I don't have that in my bank account. Do you?"

"I can chip in about a grand, that's all I have in my savings," Oscar said.

"It's a start," Doyle said just as the front door opened and in walked Poppy. "Oops, I don't have a contractor yet," Doyle said quietly to the men. Marge was back at her desk and greeted Poppy.

Doyle stood and went to her. "I haven't heard from you, are you avoiding me?" she asked him.

"Avoiding you…never. I've talked to my sheriff friend and he is supposed to talk to his brother-in-law about the building quote. I haven't heard from him though."

"Don't sweat it. I talked to him already. Your sheriff friend gave him my card and he called me this morning," she said sweetly. I have a check for you to cover rebuilding the cabin and it also covers the contents of the building." She held out a check and Doyle took it.

He looked at it and smiled. He turned back to Oscar, "Well, we have some funds to start with."

*

Chapter 19

"You're not going to throw a party with this money, are you?" Poppy asked.

Doyle laughed and said, "No, we just needed a little cash to fool some terrorist. Just enough to make it look like we have two millions dollars."

"Seeding a suitcase with money on top and paper on the bottom, eh?" she replied.

"Something like that, for just a quick scam. We're trying to recover some stolen Egyptian statues. We know they have them, so we offered to buy them. Which is where this money will come in."

"You show them the cash and they take you to the booty," she said. "Will the two of you be able to handle terrorists?"

"I've handled terrorists before. Ten years' worth of it. These guys don't seem all that tough," Doyle said.

"Famous last words. Where do you want to have your body delivered?" she replied with a laugh.

"Oh, ye of little faith. Do you want to tag along to guard the money? You seem to be tough enough to handle it."

"I can. What's your plan?"

"Probably plan B," Oscar mumbled.

"Hey, it works. Now we need to prepare the cash. I'll go to my bank and cash this, if they have enough money to handle it. I only need enough to cover the paper. Oscar, grab a couple reams of white paper from the supply cabinet and start cutting it to size. I'll be back shortly," he said and went out the back door.

Poppy looked at Oscar and said, "Shall we start cutting?"

Doyle's Quest

An hour later, they had stuffed an old suitcase Doyle had in the back, with bundles of paper topped by a number of real $100 bills.

"Think it will fool them?" Doyle asked Poppy.

"Only if they're really stupid."

"You're a ball of sunshine. They only have to get a quick look," he said with a laugh. "Now we have to wait for them to call."

Poppy and Doyle were sitting at his desk, and Oscar was visiting with Marge. They sat talking while waiting patiently for a phone call from the Nile Liberators.

"So, these terrorists need money to supposedly buy a bomb? Only one? What could they do with that?" Poppy asked.

"I don't have all the answers, just a sketch of information I got from various sources. Maybe we'll get them to talk when we meet with them."

Poppy was toying with Doyle's Indiana Jones hat. She put it on her head. "How do I look?"

"Hardly like Harrison Ford. But you look good."

"Maybe I'll buy the female version of this hat."

"They have one?" Doyle asked.

"It's actually a bush hat from Australia. Looks like this hat but different. Wider brim."

"Well, I'll take you to Harry the Hatter and buy you one. Then we can go on a dig in Egypt."

Doyle almost jumped when the burn phone buzzed on his desk. He signaled to Oscar to come over and picked up the phone.

"Hello, Holmes here," he answered as he put it on speaker.

"Mr. Holmes, my people won't sell the statues for less than two million dollars. It's our final offer. Can your client handle that?"

Doyle paused for effect, then said, "I talked to him and he agreed. I have the money with me now. Do you have all of the statues?"

"Well, there's a problem. About an hour ago, we found out the man we hired to liberate the real statues from the Wittington was taken into custody by the Detroit Police. We don't know how much he has revealed, so we are holding off moving the statues until we find out what was said. We'll contact you in a day or two," the voice said and hung up.

Doyle's Quest

"Damn, they found out about Rossi. I need to call Harry Lowe and see if we can get Rossi released from custody for the sting. Rossi knows the fake name I gave so he doesn't know who Doyle is. He can't slip that to the liberators."

"But he knows you by sight. Hopefully he won't be around to see you," Oscar said.

"They hired him to steal the statues, he's just a thief, so I don't see why they would have him included in the deal. We'll just have to play it by ear," Doyle replied. "Now we have to wait until they call in a day or two. If I can get Rossi released, they may relax, if Lowe hasn't let on about the statues. I'll call him and find out what he did."

Doyle took out his cell phone and speed dialed Detective Lowe. He put the phone on speaker after he contacted the station operator. He waited for Lowe to come on.

"You have a suspect in our holding cell, Doyle. When are you going to come in so we can get him into booking?" came a voice from the tiny speaker. "I still haven't formally charged him, because I don't know what to charge him with. I'll have to release him soon."

"Perfect. Go ahead and release him, but warn him he's not off the hook for theft. I have a problem and he's the log jam right now," Doyle spoke into the phone.

"You just want to make me work. What's the problem?"

Doyle gave him the Reader's Digest version of the problem leaving out minor details. "So, if you didn't talk to him or charge him with thefts of the statues, he may not spook the people who I'm trying to buy the objects from."

"He has no real idea why we are holding him. I haven't talked to him, I was waiting for you to explain what he's here for, officially. I'll cut him loose, just hope he doesn't queer your deal."

"Thanks Harry. Oh, and Mahmoud was perfect for the job. I'll need him one more time when we go to buy the statues. Thanks for recommending him."

"Yeah, you'll pay for that. Now I have to go let Rossi out. Talk later." He hung up and Doyle clicked off the speaker.

"Now we wait until they call. Hopefully Rossi will give them some BS about being caught by a P.I. hired by the Wittington to find the statues. But since he wasn't charged, the Liberators may feel safe."

"I don't know. I think Rossi could still screw up the deal. Just the fact that the Wittington knew the statues were stolen and hired you to find them, may make you a suspect to them."

"I'd call them back if I could, but they blocked their number. So I don't know where they are, or how to reach them."

"That woman at the consulate knew how to reach them," Oscar said.

"True, if we don't hear from them by tomorrow, we may need to pay a visit to her." He looked at Poppy, "You could go talk to her as an investigator from the insurance company covering the thefts and threaten her. We could watch her that way and see what she does. It may also speed up the sale. They'd want to get rid of the goods before they get caught."

"I love undercover work. I'd be more than happy to help," she said.

Doyle smiled when she said undercover, thinking about his late night visit to her apartment. He was hoping to repeat that night sometime soon.

"Well, not much more to do until they call. I'll carry the burn phone and if I hear from them, I'll give everyone a shout. Let's call it a day and go get some rest." He winked at Poppy and she gave him a grin.

Oscar and Marge were out the door quickly. Doyle and Poppy lingered until it was quiet in the office. "Feel like having a nice sit-down dinner somewhere?" he asked her.

"No take-out this time? I still have a bunch of containers of Chinese food in my refrigerator that I've been munching on."

"I never cared much for Chinese food, let's go find a nice steak to devour."

"If you're paying, I'm fine with it."

"Is that all I'm good for, paying for your meal?"

"That's just the beginning of what you are good for. We'll discuss that later," she said and stood, putting the Indy hat on Doyle. He stood and took her hand, kissing her lightly.

They went out to their cars and Poppy followed Doyle to his apartment before going to a restaurant. Doyle was wondering what the Nile Liberators were up to now.

*

Chapter 20

"So tell me about yourself, we didn't talk much the other night," Poppy asked as they sat at a table in the London Chop House on the corner of Congress and Shelby.

"I think we were a little too busy the other night to talk. But, how far back do you want me to go? I grew up in Oxford, Michigan, as you probably already know. I wasn't too bad in school, I had a number of friends and one girlfriend who I found out last month was murdered by the serial killer who blew up my cabin."

"How awful. The girlfriend's death, not the cabin. But that was awful, too."

"Yes, they both were. She was a pain in the rear, but she didn't deserve to die," he said with a frown. "After I graduated from high school, I went into the FBI and was recruited into their terrorist task force, black ops as I liked to call it. Although we didn't have many terrorists back then, pre 9-11, we just hunted enemies of the country. Mostly spies from Russia and mercenaries in South America. I served ten years there and then went into local law enforcement on the Detroit Police force. Where I retired from earlier this year."

"When you nearly killed the mayor," she said with a grin.

"I wasn't even close to killing him. I just gave him a small scar. I'm a fantastic shot, but he moved too quickly. He did apologize for the way he treated me after he was hit. So I left the DPD and got my private papers and opened my firm. Oscar retired from the DPD, joined me and we've been doing fairly well. Not making a lot of money right now, but hopefully things will get better when I recover the statues. There's a hefty recovery fee involved."

"So you have a lot riding on finding the statues?"

"You could say that. If these Nile turkeys would get their act together, we can bring this to a close."

"What if they give you a fight?"

"Oscar and I are both armed and ready for the worst. I've dealt with bad guys that would make these people look like Disneyland employees."

"I like a confident man. As I said, I'll be glad to help out."

"You could wear something low cut and short to distract them. While Oscar and I hit them quickly."

Doyle's Quest

"I'm not a sex object, I can fight just as well. I have a third-dan black belt in Judo and I'm proficient in Krav Maga."

"You worked with the Israeli forces to train?" Doyle asked.

"No, I had an instructor here. He was with the Israeli Security Agency for a lot of years before he retired and took me in to learn. I'm pretty dangerous according to him."

"Yes, I've seen a few of those moves in bed," Doyle said and smiled.

"I've got moves you haven't even seen yet."

"Well, I don't want to wolf down this great steak, but I'm ready to go again."

"Just be patient. You'll be rewarded," she said with a gleam in her eyes.

An hour and a half later, they were wrestling in bed, showing their hand to hand combat moves. Poppy managed to pin Doyle down and he yielded. The rest of the night was less violent.

The next morning, Doyle struggled out of the bedroom and into the bath. He found Poppy standing in the shower with the curtain open. "About time you got here," she laughed and pulled him in.

Since neither ate breakfast, they dressed and went out to their cars. "Better if you follow. I don't know what's going to happen today," he said.

She went to her car and drove out behind Doyle. They arrived at the office and parked. In the office, Marge and Oscar were relaxing watching TV.

"Nothing better to do, guys?" Doyle asked.

"Just waiting for our fearless leader to arrive. Heard anything from the bad guys?" Oscar said.

"Nothing yet. I'm hoping Rossi didn't screw up our deal. I guess we'll see today."

"Poppy, good morning," Oscar said when she came up. "I presume you had a restful night?"

"You could say that," was all she admitted to.

"Is your schedule clear?" Doyle asked Oscar.

"No cheating spouses to chase. So I'm good to go."

Doyle went to his desk and put the burn phone down. He sat and Poppy sat on his client chair. Doyle put his hat on the desk and sat back. "This is as bad as being on the force. Sit and wait for something to happen. Although I had a commander who didn't like his men sitting around. He always found grunt jobs for us to do, so we welcomed crime to strike."

"I called my office this morning and took a couple days off. I didn't say why, they didn't ask. Most of the men don't like a woman investigator, so they don't care if I'm absent."

"Well, I think women cops are just as good as the men. Better in some instances," Doyle said just as his personal cell phone rang out the *Jaws* theme. Poppy laughed when she heard it. Doyle looked at the Caller ID and saw it was Wendy. He figured it would be better to move away from Poppy to take the call. He excused himself and went to the back of the office.

"Hey, Wendy, what's happening?" he said when he answered.

"I just thought I'd call to see if we were still friends," she said.

"I have no problems with us. I'd still like to see you, but I'm going to be tied up for a few days on a case. I can give you a call this weekend and maybe we can do something then."

"I won't hold you to that, but it would be nice to see you. I got a call from my lawyer and he said the bar is going to settle out of court. So I may have money now to live on and take care of getting my legs fixed."

"That would be great. Where would you have the surgery?"

"Probably Henry Ford Hospital. They have good surgeons there."

"Well, let me know when and I'll be there for you."

"Thanks, I'll let you go back to work. I just wanted to let you know about my lawsuit. Give me a call when you can, I hope you do."

"You'll hear from me, definitely. I'll call. Take care." They finished and he hung up. He stood looking at his phone thinking about Wendy. She was really a good person, just had an agenda that was a little shady. But it was only to better herself. He actually liked her, she seemed special and he enjoyed the time he spent with her. He turned and saw Poppy sitting next to his desk. Now she was a different story.

"Sorry about that, personal call from a friend," he said as he went back to his desk. "Now, where were we?"

"You were talking about how women cops were just as good as men cops."

Doyle's Quest

"Yes, and I meant it. I had a woman partner when I was patrolling the streets. She pulled me out of a few scrapes. She went on to work in the Organized Crime Unit, undercover in gangs around Detroit. She was a mean bitch when she wanted," Doyle said with a laugh.

"You talking about Phoebe Wiscoski?" Oscar said as he came over.

"Did you know her?" Doyle asked.

"She was well known to most of the department. I heard she retired last year. She said her body couldn't take much more of the undercover gang life."

"Undercover can change a cop. It's hard on them having to pretend to go along with the BS they do. In the past I've pretended to be someone I wasn't for a sting, but never to live with the scum like undercover cops do."

The burn phone on Doyle's desk suddenly buzzed. Everyone stared at it, then Doyle picked it up. He hit answer and speaker, then said, "Yeah, Holmes here."

"Okay, we took care of our man who was arrested. He won't be giving any trouble for us now," came the voice from the phone.

174

"What are you talking about? What did you do?" Doyle asked.

"Don't you worry about that, he's no problem for us now. We have business to take care of. Do you still have the money?"

Doyle felt mixed about Rossi. Was he killed by the Liberators? "Look, I'm open to buying your objects, but my client and I don't want to be involved in some murder. The man you said stole the statues for you, is he still alive?"

"Why should you care? He was nothing to you."

"As I said, it's bad enough buying stolen artifacts from the Egyptians, but to have murder attached to it, not good for business."

There was a pause, then the man said, "He's still alive, we have been questioning him about his stay in the police station. We are satisfied he revealed nothing."

"Well, if you want the money, he better not be harmed. My client won't go for being part of murder, even if he wants the statues."

"We won't harm him. Just relocate him from here. Is that good enough?"

Doyle hoped he was being truthful, but knew these animals weren't to be trusted. "Okay, I'll take your word for it. Now how do you want to do the exchange? I expect all the statues to be there and my appraiser will examine each one to be sure we are getting the real deal, understood. Then you get the money."

"We agree."

*

Chapter 21

"Where shall we meet?" Doyle asked, hoping it would be somewhere out in the open.

"You know where Michigan Central Station is?" the voice asked.

"The rundown train station and office building that's been closed down for years? That Central Station?"

"The same. Go to the front of the building and you'll find the fence is cut open by the gate. Go in and through the front entrance. Then go to the ticket counter, what's left of it, and wait. Tomorrow at noon. Be there with the money and your appraiser. We'll wait for you for only a half hour before we leave, so be on time," he said and then hung up.

Doyle sat back, thinking, then said, "If they have all the statues, they won't be able to move very fast with all those heavy objects. So I'm sure they'll wait for us, but we'll be on time."

"Michigan Central Station. That's a dangerous building, it's huge and falling apart," Oscar said.

"In its heyday it was the tallest train station in the world. It's had many owners since, including Amtrak, but the last twenty years or so it's been abandoned and falling apart. The only thing saving it from being blown up is that it was declared an historic site. They called it the Ellis Island of Detroit with people from all over the world coming into the city by train."

"Now it's a place for vagrants, teenagers and vandals to hangout. The guy who owns it says he wants to fix it up, but he makes a lot of promises," Poppy said.

Doyle looked at her, "You know the place?"

"I do. I used to sneak in with friends and we'd explore. It had to have been a beautiful place when it was still open to the public," she said.

"It was. As a boy my dad would take me there after a ball game at Tiger stadium to watch the trains come and go."

"Why would they want to meet there with the statues?" Oscar said.

"I have no idea, and I don't care as long as they have the statues," Doyle replied.

"Maybe it's where they're hiding out," Oscar said. "Lot's of places to stash the goods. I knew a perp we were chasing who disappeared into the station to hide. We had no idea where to find him. That place has lots of underground rooms and tunnels."

Doyle sat staring out the front window. "They want to meet tomorrow, maybe we need to explore the place today."

Oscar laughed and said, "Put your Indy hat on and let's go explore the tombs."

Doyle looked at Poppy. "Feel like going on a dig?"

She grinned, and stood. "I'm ready, I even wore my exploring clothes." She was dressed down in slacks and a heavy bush shirt.

Doyle put on his hat, stood and said to Marge, "If we're needed, take a message and tell them to come back." Then he turned to Oscar and Poppy, "Let's go."

The three left the building and went to Doyle's car. The distance to the station wasn't that far, less than half a mile, so it didn't take long.

"Interesting that we don't have to travel far through Detroit to deal with these people," Oscar said from the back seat.

"Too convenient, I'd say, but I don't think they know anything about us." Doyle replied. "I was the one who set up the first meet at the ball park with us, they told us to go to the station. So it's just coincidence that it's so close."

Doyle pulled up to the side of the building outside the fence along Vernor Highway, that was supposed to be keeping the building safe from vandals. They got out and Doyle said to walk to the front of the building where the fence opening was supposed to be.

Everyone was looking up at the eighteen stories of former offices above the train station. Just about all the window had been busted out giving the massive wall a desolate war-torn look. They came to an opening in the fence that looked like someone had cut the wire.

Doyle's Quest

"This worries me. I hope they don't have armed guards in there," Oscar said.

"Now why would they? The building is empty and I'm sure stripped of all the metals that can be sold. Armed guards would be overkill," Doyle replied.

"Maybe they have vicious guard dogs? Like German Shepherds or Dobermans," Poppy offered with a chuckle.

Doyle looked back at her, "You're not helping the situation. I'm sure there isn't anything in here that will hurt us."

"Other than the Nile Liberators," Oscar mumbled.

"If you want to go back to the car, go ahead. I won't stop you," Doyle said as he went up to the front entrance followed by his friends.

The wide door was blocked by an iron gate that was rusting but still standing.

"I guess we can't go through that," Oscar said.

Doyle reached out and pulled on the gate, it swung back with a creaking noise. "I guess we can."

Doyle turned to Poppy, "You still want to join us?"

"Lead on, Indy," she said with a smile.

They entered the building to what had to have been the main waiting room. It reminded Doyle of an ancient Roman bathhouse with marble floors and vaulted ceiling. Moving along quietly, they came to a large hall adorned with columns that led to the ticket office and what once were the arcade shops. Beyond that was the concourse with brick walls and a large copper skylight, from which passengers would walk down a ramp to the departing trains. At one time, there were eleven tracks, but they're all deserted now, and most of the tracks were torn up. Doyle had heard that below the whole structure were large areas for baggage, mail handling and offices. A person could get lost easily down there.

Doyle stopped before the ticket counter and looked around.

"It's scary quiet in here," Oscar said.

"No traffic nearby and no people meandering around to make noise. The only sounds you might hear are birds and animals. Shall we explore?"

They spent the better part of two hours going through the building. They found nothing much to suggest that the Nile Liberators were hiding in the building.

They were going down a hallway in the office tower when Doyle heard a noise. He went to the door that he heard the noise coming from. He and Oscar pulled their guns as Doyle slowly turned the knob. He carefully pushed the door open then shoved it, as they both rushed in with their guns out front.

A girl screamed as they entered. Doyle stood looking at two teenagers on a blanket in the middle of the room. They were almost naked. Oscar laughed quietly behind Doyle and Poppy moved around to see what was going on. She smiled at the two now trying to get dressed quickly.

"Hey, man. Don't shoot. We weren't doing anything wrong," the young boy stammered.

Now Doyle was trying not to laugh. "Not yet you weren't. We're not here to shoot you or arrest you. Finish getting dressed and you can answer a few questions."

Doyle went to a table which had a few chairs still unbroken near it. He pulled two of them next to each other and stood back. The young couple finished getting dressed and Doyle motioned for them to sit on the chairs.

"Now if you would, please answer a few questions for us," Doyle asked.

The boy shook his head quickly, "Anything you need to know, mister."

"How long have you been in here?"

"Since this morning. We were playing around the building and then came in here," the boy answered.

"Just today?"

"No, we come here a lot. It's a big building, so there's lots to see. I take pictures too. I'm sort of a photo bug."

"Have you seen any suspicious activity involving men with boxes or crates?"

Now the boy looked spooked. "You mean the evil looking guys?"

"Evil? How so?"

"They looked like terrorists, Arabic types. We saw them yesterday when we were hiding in the big room behind the pews."

"What were they doing?"

"They were going in and out of the ticket office. There's an entrance into more offices from that room. It also leads to the lower levels where we went once, but never again. It's really scary down there."

"Did they carry anything with them?"

"They had small cases, like packing boxes for small things. There were about nine of them. I counted."

"They took them through the ticket office?"

"Yeah, they had a flatbed cart that they brought them in with."

"When was this?"

"Yesterday, around noon."

"Don't you two have school to go to?" Poppy asked.

They looked at her and the girl said, "School is out for fall break."

"Ah, I see. Did the men leave the building?" she asked.

"Yeah, they did. Karen and I went into see what they left, but we didn't want to go in the basement."

184

"They're still down there?" Doyle asked.

"As far as we know, yes," the boy replied.

"Did you see the men today?"

"Not while we were here. We didn't go looking for them. We came up here to be away from them if they came back."

"Okay, those men are very dangerous. They wouldn't hesitate to kill you two. So I would suggest you get out of here quickly," Doyle said and waited for them to move, they didn't. "I'm not going to repeat it, get out of here, now!" he said louder.

The two looked at each other and then ran out the door. Oscar and Poppy laughed. Doyle just smiled.

"Okay, shall we go see if the boxes are still there?"

*

Chapter 22

The three of them went to the stairs going back down to the first floor level. Doyle led them back around to the ticket office hoping the statues were still stored there. They entered the room and found nothing.

"Okay, they either have them in another room, or removed them for some reason," Doyle said.

"If they wanted us to see them tomorrow, then it would stand to reason they would leave them here," Oscar said.

"True, no sense in moving them around, especially with the weight they must be. Let's go down that hallway and check the rooms." They went door to door checking each room, but found nothing.

There was one door at the end of the hall that had a padlock on it. "Now why would there be a locked door in an abandoned building?" Doyle asked rhetorically. "I don't really want to break the lock, it would give it away that we were here."

"Don't you think with all the vandals that go through this building, someone would break in?" Poppy asked. "They couldn't assume it was us."

"True," Doyle said, "but I would think they'd realize that vandals could break in and grab their stash. There must be something more to this door than we see."

"Think it might be booby trapped?" Oscar asked.

Doyle was examining the door closely looking for wires or micro-switches. He saw none then examined the lock. "If I had a bump key we could get in without breaking the lock."

Poppy reached into her pocket and came out with a key. "You mean like this bump key?"

Doyle was amazed. "Why do you have a bump key?"

"Don't ask, it's personal," she replied with a sly smile.

"You are a scary person," he said taking the key from her.

"I'm only scary if you piss me off," she laughed. She bent down and picked up a small brick that must have been used to prop the door open. "Here, you can use this to hit it."

Doyle's Quest

Doyle took the brick and then inserted the key in the lock. He whacked the key a couple times until he felt the tumblers give. He pulled on it and the lock opened.

"You're good at that, I may need you next time I use the key," she said.

"I used to carry a bump key when I was a detective, just in case I needed to break and enter without a warrant." He winked at her and removed the lock from the hasp. "Okay, both of you stand way back. I'm going to open the door and back up quickly in case."

"Remember to duck in case they have a shotgun or explosive planted," Oscar said.

Poppy and Oscar went back down the hall as Doyle turned the door knob and opened it carefully a crack. He looked up and down to see if there were any wires attached, but saw none. He stood with his back to the wall and gave the door a good shove then dropped down. The door swung open and nothing happened.

He stood as Poppy and Oscar came up. "These guys are either real dumb or trusting," he said. They looked past the door and found it was a stairway going down.

"Didn't the kid upstairs say it was spooky down there?" Oscar asked.

"Spooky doesn't bother me, it's men with guns that do," Doyle said. "You can wait here if spooky bothers you."

"No, I'll go down since we are armed."

"I'm not," Poppy said.

Doyle looked back at her and asked, "Have you ever used a gun?"

"Yes, I was trained to attack a man holding a gun, take it away from him and shoot him with it. Is that close enough?"

Doyle just grinned, then said, "You are scary." He reached under his jacket to the back of his belt and took out the .38 Smith and Wesson he carried there as a backup.

"I'd rather have that Sig you carry under your arm. I like big guns," she said with another sly grin.

Doyle pulled the gun from its shoulder holster and said, "No one but me gets to play with my big gun."

"I got to play with your big gun the other night," she said in his ear.

189

Doyle's Quest

"Let's keep the conversation to the immediate situation." He handed her the .38 and said, "Don't shoot me in the back, please."

Doyle turned to the stairway landing and went in. There was a switch on the wall, he flipped it but nothing happened. "I didn't figure there was electricity, but hey, it was worth a try." He went down after taking out the small but powerful flashlight from another pocket. The stairs were old and creaky.

"If they brought the statues down here, I'm surprised these stairs didn't break under the weight," Doyle said.

They got to the bottom and they were looking down another hallway. There were only three doors off the hallway, they went to the first. Doyle carefully opened it and found no boxes. The room looked a shambles, and it must have been a mail room for the building as there were many walls of pigeon holes for mail. They went to the next one and found nothing also. The last door was at the end of the hall.

"If there's no boxes in here, I'd say they hid the boxes very well," Doyle said. He was just about to turn the knob when they heard a voice behind them.

They looked back at a man carrying an old Russian AK-47 assault rifle, aimed at them. "I wouldn't do that," he said in broken English. He moved closer, holding the rifle on them.

Doyle whispered to Poppy, "This is where you take the gun from the man and shoot him with it."

"He's too far away and the hallway is too narrow to do my fancy acrobatics," she whispered back.

"Shut up and put any weapons on the floor," he yelled waving the rifle up and down.

"Okay, take it easy with that thing. It could go off accidently," Doyle said.

"I know how to use this. I trained well. Now drop your weapons. And also your cell phones."

They carefully set the guns on the floor and then took out their cell phones. Doyle reached in and took out the burn phone he still carried, leaving his good cell phone in his pocket. He set it on the floor next to his gun.

"Now open the door and go in, don't make any fast moves or I'll shoot the person closest to me. It will be the woman."

Doyle turned back to the door and finished opening it. The room was dark and smelled bad. The man yelled to go in, they did. The man reached to the wall and flipped a switch and there was light. Doyle wondered how he managed that. Then he saw a large battery box on the floor with wires running to the lights above.

The man said, "You will stay in here until my superior comes. He will deal with you."

"How did you know we were down here?" Doyle asked stalling for time.

"We have sensors. They send a signal to me upstairs and I come down here."

"Where were you upstairs? We searched the building," Doyle asked.

"You didn't search very well. I was in a small room waiting for my comrades to return. You stay in here now." He backed out of the room closing the door. They could hear it locking.

Doyle went to the door and there was a crack in the door jamb that he could see through. The man bent down and picked up the guns and phones and then went off to the stairs.

"Great, we could break the door but he'd just come back and shoot us," Oscar said.

"Never fear, my friend. I have a plan," Doyle said. He took out his cell phone and looked at his contact list.

"You gave him the burn phone," Oscar said with a smile. "Are you calling the police?"

"No, I don't want them to get involved with the statues," he said as he pointed behind Oscar. There were a stack of packing crates in the corner the room. "I'm calling in some troops since I know that the statues are here." He dialed a number and waited.

"Who you calling?" Oscar asked.

"Remember Monk?"

"From the Cass Street motorcycle gang?"

"Yep. They can get here fast and we don't have to involve the cops." He paused when he heard someone answer. "Monk, Art Doyle here. Got a minute to talk?" He listened, then said, "Yeah, that Doyle. I need a favor."

Doyle explained where they were and the situation. "Be careful, this guy has an AK-47. Just keep an eye out for him. Oh and do you have access to a truck?" He listened then said, "Good, bring it. I need some crates moved. Thanks, man." He hung up and smiled. "The army is on the way."

About twenty minutes later they could hear a scream and a couple gun shots. Then someone yelled at the locked door. "You in there Doyle?" came a booming voice.

"We are, is that you Monk?" Doyle replied.

"At your service, stand back away from the door."

Doyle moved everyone away from the door as a gun blast blew the lock out. Monk kicked in the door and lumbered in. "Room service," he said with a grin, then he went to Doyle and gave him a bear hug.

*

Chapter 23

"Monk, good to see you," Doyle said as he took a big breath when Monk released him from the hug.

"Monk, you should remember Oscar and this is Poppy Drake, insurance investigator."

"Pleasure to meet you Poppy. Nice Doyle, do all you P.I. types have good-looking women around?"

"When we can, yes," Doyle replied with a grin.

"I heard what you did to Skeeter, I'm proud of you, man. Now what do you need moved?" he replied.

"Well, saving us came first, what did you do with the man upstairs?"

"Oh, he may not walk too straight for a while, but he's alive. You want we should make him disappear?"

"No, just keep him out of sight for a few days. The stuff I want moved are those boxes over there," he said, pointing to the crates. "You did bring a few men?"

He turned and yelled out the door, "Wolf, bring the guys down here."

A couple seconds later, a half dozen or so men came into the room. Big, hulking men, looking from out of a psycho motorcycle movie. Monk pointed to the crates. "Get these boxes upstairs and out to the truck."

"They're heavy and don't drop them," Doyle added.

Doyle led Oscar, Poppy and Monk out of the room as the men started to remove the crates. They went upstairs where Doyle recovered their guns and cell phones then went out to the parking lot where the men had parked the truck.

"How did you get the truck so close to the building?" Doyle asked.

"We rammed a fence around the side," he grinned.

"I won't turn you in," Doyle said. He looked to the back of the truck where the men were putting the crates in. The lone Nile hood was tied up in the back of the truck looking scared. Doyle asked if they had a hammer or crowbar. Monk went up to the cab of the truck and took out a tool box. He brought a crowbar back to Doyle.

Doyle took the crowbar to the one crate on the ground and pried the top up. Inside, packed in plastic peanuts, was a statue. He put the top back down and used the crowbar to drive the nails back in.

There were four motorcycles parked around the truck as Doyle asked, "Did you break any laws driving the truck here, besides destroying a fence?"

"We didn't want to attract any cops, so we drove safely. Now, where do you want us to take the boxes?"

"Down Michigan Avenue a short ways, just past the old Tiger Stadium, to my office. I'll lead you to it."

They had the last crate put into the truck and Doyle went to get his car. He had them follow him to his office and around to the back door. Oscar said, as he got out of the car, "You know those Nile people will be pissed when they find the statues missing."

"I'm counting on it. I'm sure they won't know who has the goods, but they may figure it out. I'm sure I'll get a call." Monk came up and asked what to do with the crates. "Bring them inside here," Doyle said and pointed to his back door. He went to unlock the door and went in.

Marge saw him come in and went to him. "Arthur, I got a call from Mr. Charles at the gallery. He said two men came in and were asking about who he hired to investigate the missing statues. Is that important?"

Doyle thought on it a moment then said, "Thanks Marge, it could be important." He turned to Oscar, "No one knew I was investigating except Harry Lowe. The only other person was Rossi, after I told him I was investigating for the gallery. He didn't know my name so maybe he mentioned to the Nile people about me. They went to Charles and asked who I was. They may come here next." Doyle went back out to Monk standing by the truck waiting for his men to start moving the crates.

"Monk, change of plan. Can you take the crates to my storage over on Cass by your club house? Xtra Room Storage, Unit 79, here's the key," he said taking the key off his keyring. "There should be enough space to put them in. I'll let you know what is going to happen and I may need you back here without the truck."

"Anything you need, man. We can take the crates there and drop off the truck. You want us to come back here?"

"Not all of you, just a couple of your best men, with their toys of destruction. Bring a couple cars, no motorcycles."

"Gotcha. We'll be back shortly," Monk said and told his men of the change of plan.

Doyle watched them drive away. Poppy came up behind him. "Think the liberators will pay you a visit?"

"I'm sure they will. Especially after they find their stash is gone. Let's go inside and plan."

Oscar and Marge were talking as Doyle and Poppy came up. "They must know where we are by now. Marge said Charles gave them your name. He asked if that was all right."

"A little late to ask that, but we have to be prepared now," Doyle said. "Monk is coming back with a couple of his men and I'll station them outside the building, front and back. Do you still have those walkie-talkies?"

"I do," he said and went to his desk.

Doyle turned to Marge, "I think you need to take the rest of the day off, for your own safety."

"I have my .357 with me," she said.

"And I'm sure you can handle it, but I'd feel better if you weren't here. Please go home, for me."

She smiled and said she would. She gathered her things and gave Doyle a kiss on the cheek. "You're the son I never had," she said and went out the back door.

Doyle turned to Poppy and she said to him, "You're not getting rid of me that easily. I'm liking your dangerous lifestyle, so I'm staying for the duration. Besides, I already took a couple days off of work."

"You still have my .38, don't lose it. And don't shoot me if there's gun play."

Doyle's Quest

"Will you stop worrying about your gun and your butt. I know what I'm doing." She gave him a kiss on the other cheek. "Now, what is your plan?"

Doyle stood by his desk thinking about what may happen. "I'll have Monk's men outside in their cars with the walkie-talkies and if the Nile people come in, I'll signal the Calvary to come in behind them. Have your guns ready for anything." He went to the back where the boxes of equipment was stored. He opened a box and took out three Kevlar vests and handed them to Oscar and Poppy. "Put these on just in case."

"How many of these do you have and where'd you get them?" Oscar asked.

"I sort of collected them when I was on the PD. Don't ask, just wear them."

They put the vests on under their jackets and went back to Doyle's desk. About a half hour later Monk walked in the back door.

"I got four men with me, in two of their cars out back. What do you want us to do?"

Doyle handed him two walkie-talkies and said to give them to the men and have one car out front and one in back, then be ready to come running in case of trouble.

"We can do that," the big man said. "We love trouble."

"Come back in here and wait with us," Doyle asked.

"Will do," he said and went out the back door again.

"It's been a couple hours since the men visited Charles. So it should come down to a visit soon," Doyle said. "I'm hoping they visited the Station to find their cargo gone. That should rile them up."

"Today is not a good day to die," Oscar said.

"No day is, so let's be real careful. I don't know how dangerous these people are, but from the ones I saw the other day at our first meeting, they looked dangerous. Let's relax until something happens."

About twenty minutes later, they were relaxing as Doyle told Monk about what happened with Skeeter. "Too bad about your cabin, man, but no crying for the loss of that bastard."

Doyle was about to answer him when his desk phone rang. He knew that the Nile people wouldn't have his cell phone number so they must have looked his office phone number up. He picked up the receiver and hit speaker. "Hello, Doyle and Drew Investigations."

"I presume you are Doyle?" came a voice from the phone speaker.

"I am, and who am I speaking to?" Doyle said, recognizing the voice from the last conversation on a phone.

"I think you know who we are. You have been very bad to mess with our plans. I suspect you are the person who inquired about buying the statues also. Clever plan to track down our property."

"It's not your property. The statues belong to the Egyptian people."

"We had possession, so it is ours. Now it seems you have the objects. We want them back."

"Well, it was my job to return the statues to the gallery. But I think I'll see they get back to the Egyptian consulate. Then it will be their problem."

"Mr. Doyle, we want the statues back now. You will regret it if you don't return them."

"Yeah? Well come and get them," Doyle said and hung up.

"Well, that should really piss them off." Oscar said with a smirk.

*

Chapter 24

Oscar was watching out the front window and said, "They must have called from nearby, here they come." He moved over beside Monk as he stood, holding on to his weapon, a sawed-off shotgun.

The door opened and Monk said into his walkie-talkie to be ready. Doyle stood and came forward of everyone. There were four of them, with a nicely-dressed man in the lead. "I presume you are the head of the Nile Liberators?"

The man gave him an icy stare. "I'm one of them. We number in hundreds around the world. Our local group here is ready to go fight the government of Egypt."

"Kind of far from your government aren't you?" Doyle asked keeping his hand ready to go for his Sig.

"There are Egyptian agencies and people in all countries that need to be dealt with. We are here to take care of the American loving Egyptians. You have messed with our plan and we want the statues back now."

"But who's going to buy them to front your bomb buying effort?"

"We have interested parties. They want to take the prizes of Egypt away to make them suffer at the loss."

"Then you'll buy your bomb, probably an old Russian WMD bomb, and destroy, what, the consulate?"

"We will do more harm than that, Mr. Doyle. There is an Egyptian festival in Dearborn soon that will, how you say, be a blast."

"Aren't you worried that by telling us, we'll spoil your fun?"

"No, you will not live to tell anyone."

"What makes you think that?"

"We have your receptionist. She will die if my man doesn't hear from me in…" he looked at his watch, "…in twenty minutes." He stood smiling. "You will take us to the statues and then we will kill you, so you won't spoil our fun."

Doyle looked quickly to Oscar and said to call Marge. He picked up the phone on Doyle's desk and dialed. Doyle was getting pissed now. He let Marge go out into a trap.

Oscar said there was no answer. Doyle moved towards the man and said, "If you hurt her you'll be the first to die of your motley scum of a terrorist group." Doyle brought out his Sig and aimed it at the man. The other three men pulled assault weapons out of their long coats. The leader held his hand up and the men stopped.

"He will not harm me," he said to his men. "He wants his old woman to live. Americans are so sensitive about family and friends. Are you not, Mr. Doyle?"

Doyle's phone buzzed in his pocket and he pulled it out. It was Marge, according to the caller ID. He turned and held it to his ear and said quietly, "Are you all right?"

He heard Marge say, "I'm fine, Arthur. I had a funny feeling something was up, so when I got home I took out my gun and waited at the back door. A man came in and I cold-cocked him with the gun. He's tied up in my kitchen right now. Is everyone all right there?"

Doyle got a wide grin and said, "We're good. Keep him tied up, we'll come to get him in a while."

Doyle's Quest

Doyle hung up and quietly told Oscar that Marge had the situation in hand. Then he looked at Monk and said to call his men in. Monk made the call as Doyle turned back to the man. "I don't think we'll take you to the statues. You need to surrender now before this gets messy."

"I don't appreciate your flippant attitude, Mr. Doyle. You don't understand the danger you are in."

"No, *you* don't understand," he said as the front door flew opened and in came the bikers with their shotguns out. They stood their ground as the back door opened and the others came in. Oscar, Monk and Poppy had their guns up and ready now also.

"Feeling a little outnumbered?" Doyle asked, bringing his Sig to the man's throat. Doyle looked to the Nile hoods and said, "You can lower your weapons now."

The bikers went to the men and grabbed the guns from them. The men held their hands up and didn't fight.

"Damn, I wanted a good gunfight," Poppy said from behind Doyle.

He laughed and said, "Take two of them out to the back and shoot them, if it'll make you feel better." The men gave her a frightened stare. She brought up the .38 and grinned, then lowered it.

Doyle went to his desk and took out four zip-cuffs from a drawer and handed them to Monk. "Go strap them good, so we can hand them over to the authorities." Doyle thought about calling his FBI friend Kent again, maybe the terrorist task force would like to have these men.

Doyle went to the leader and said, "I never got your name?"

"I didn't give it, and I won't, you pig," he spat out the words.

"Gee, that's no way to talk, and here I was thinking about shooting you." He turned to Oscar and said, "Take one of Monk's men and go get the hood at Marge's place. She's got him tied up."

Monk told one of his men to go with Oscar and they left. Monk pulled the terrorist to the back of the office and told them to get down on the floor. Doyle smiled that Monk was taking so much on himself to handle the situation. Monk came to Doyle, "Now what?"

"I'm calling a friend in the FBI and see if he wants these bums. So relax and watch them."

"Will do, boss." He turned and took a chair to the back where he sat facing the men.

Poppy came up and said, "He takes his job seriously, doesn't he?"

"I wouldn't mess with him, he's good to have around," he said as he sat at his desk and took out his cell phone. Poppy sat next to his desk and listened.

"Kent, I got a present for you," he said when his friend came on. "How's a bunch of terrorists that were bent on murdering a lot of people at a festival near Detroit."

"Talk to me," Kent replied in Doyle's ear. Doyle explained more information from the last conversation he had a couple days ago.

"Interesting. I think we can take that problem off your hands," Kent replied. "I just happen to be in Detroit and I'll talk to the Special Agent in Charge and get some men over. Be patient, we're on our way."

They hung up and Doyle gave Poppy a smile. "I had expected worse. That was refreshing there was no blood shed."

"Do you think this is over?" she asked.

"I doubt it, but this part of their plot is squelched. As he said, there are others out there. It's up to the FBI to interrogate these men to find out where there are others like them. I just need to get the statues back to the gallery."

"At least you didn't lose the money I gave you to rebuild your cabin," she said eyeing the case with the cash by the desk.

"Damn, I forgot about the cabin. I need to call my sheriff friend and tell him to have his brother-in-law start building. Excuse me." He reached for the phone and called Mike Twain. He talked briefly with him and told him to get the building going. They finished up and Doyle looked at Poppy. "It's rolling. Hopefully they'll have the cabin finished before fall ends. Otherwise I'll have to pitch a tent by the lake to relax."

"I'd like to see that," Poppy said with a sly smile.

The back door flew open and Oscar came in carrying a man with the help of Monk's friend. They saw the others sitting on the floor and dropped the man by them. Oscar came over to Doyle.

"Marge is one heck of a dangerous woman. She knocked him out and hog-tied him for us. Now what?"

Doyle's Quest

"The FBI is coming to take our guests away then we'll go get the statues and return them to the gallery. Our job will be finished."

"And you didn't get to go on an expedition to Egypt with your Indy hat," Oscar said.

"That basement at the Central Station was as close to an Egyptian tomb as I want to be in. Take a break, Oscar, you need it."

Oscar nodded and pulled a chair over next to Monk and sat.

About twenty minutes later, FBI special agent Kent Simmons entered from the front followed by a team of agents. Doyle had seen the big black FBI transport van pull up and stood, greeting his friend. "Good time getting here," Doyle said.

"We're only just a couple miles away. My boss wants these men real bad. He had word that they were moving in to the city but nothing substantial as to their activities. He said to thank you for rounding them up."

"There's still one of them at the consulate. I'll give you her name so you can gather her, also."

The FBI agents moved the Liberators out of the building into the van. Doyle said goodbye to Kent and he left with his men.

"That was fast, in and out," Monk said watching the van pull away.

"The Detroit branch of the Feebies don't mess around. Now we need to go get the statues. Can you have the truck meet us at the storage unit?"

"I'll call and have it there," Monk said and pulled his cell phone.

Doyle went to Poppy and asked, "Still want to hang with us?"

"I wouldn't miss it until it's over," she said.

*

Chapter 25

Doyle, Oscar and Poppy went to Doyle's car as Monk drove off with his men, all heading for the storage unit.

"Did you call Mr. Charles at the gallery yet?" Oscar asked as they drove.

Doyle's Quest

"No, I want to drop off the statues as a surprise. This isn't over yet, and I have a feeling there's more," Doyle replied.

"You think we'll have more trouble?"

"It's just a feeling I have. So be ready for anything."

They pulled into the gated storage facility and around to Doyle's unit. The truck was already there, waiting for the statues to be loaded up. Doyle pulled up behind the truck leaving enough room to carry the crates from the unit to the truck. The cars carrying Monk and his men pulled past the truck and parked. Everyone gathered at the roll-up door of the unit as Monk took the key out of his pocket and unlocked the unit. He handed the key to Doyle and pulled up the metal door.

They stood staring at the crates just as Poppy told Doyle she had to call her office. He nodded as she went around to the front of the truck for privacy. Doyle was just about to ask Monk to have his men load the crates when they heard a vehicle coming around the row of units. It was a large pickup truck and it pulled up close to the men.

The driver jumped out with an automatic assault rifle, and from the passenger side a woman got out holding a revolver. They both aimed the weapons at Doyle and the men. Doyle realized that the woman was Irina Scoppolis from the consulate. She came forward as her man stood off the side still aiming his weapon at the men.

"Mr. Holmes, or should I say Doyle, good to see you again. I'm annoyed with your antics of tracking down our possessions. Now if you could instruct your men to load the crates into our truck, we'll leave you in peace."

"In pieces maybe. You'll move us into the unit, killing us and closing the door. How did you find us?"

"I got word at the consulate that Egyptian nationalists were being detained by the FBI and I demanded they be released to the Egyptian authorities. But your FBI said that Homeland Security had taken over the case and were keeping the men. Nevertheless, I don't need those men, I can get more. When I heard about this mess, I looked up your address and we followed you from your office to our statues. Now, if you would please load them for us in our truck."

Poppy was sitting in the passenger seat of the truck talking on her phone. She glanced in the side rear view mirror and saw Irina with a gun. She didn't know who the woman was, but knew the gun wasn't part of the plan. She hung up her phone, opened the truck door quietly, slipped out and moved stealthily along the side of the big truck. She listened to the woman explaining and decided she was not a good person.

Poppy still had Doyle's .38 and brought it out, aiming it at the woman's gun hand. She fired once then turned the gun on the man with the rifle and shot him in the thigh. The gun flew from Irina's hand and then the man went down from his wound. Monk's men jumped the two and held them.

Poppy came around and said to Doyle, "Okay, I finally got to shoot someone."

"And, I thank you for that. Now I have to bother Kent again to pick up these two. This is getting to be a busy day." Poppy gave Doyle his gun saying she was finished with it. Doyle pulled his cell phone and called Kent.

An hour later, the crates were loaded in the truck and Kent came with his men to take Irina and her henchman away. Doyle told Monk to follow him and everyone got in their vehicles and drove out from the storage facility.

They arrived around the back of the Wittington Gallery and up to the loading dock. Doyle told everyone to wait for him as he took Poppy in the building. They were in the shipping and receiving area when Len Ferigamo, head of the gallery security came rushing in. He saw Doyle and relaxed.

214

"I saw a truck pulling up to loading dock on our cameras and came running. Have you got the statues?"

"Sure do. Can you open the loading bay door?"

Len Ferigamo went to a card pad next to the door and slid his card. The huge door slowly rolled up and Monk grinned from the back of the truck. Ferigamo was surprised to see bikers standing around the crates.

"They're cool," Doyle said when he saw the concern on Ferigamo's face. "They helped save the statues. Now, I need to see Mr. Charles. Can you call him to check the cargo?"

Ferigamo smiled and went to a phone hanging on the wall. He made a call and then hung up. "Charles is on his way."

A couple minute later, as Monk's men had the crates moved to the loading bay, Charles came rushing in a door. "Mr. Doyle, thank you so much for finding the statues. I was so worried. The Egyptians are coming tomorrow to collect the statues, so this was close."

"Let's do this," Doyle said, "we'll take the real statues and replace them for the fakes, pack the fakes up and dispose of them. That way the Egyptians won't have any idea of what happened."

"Excellent idea, thank you so much. Len, have your men supervise the trading of the statues," Charles told his man.

Monk's men spent the next hour unpacking the statues as the security guards moved them to the exhibit bringing back the fakes. The fakes were put into the crates and back on the truck. Charles had his new appraiser check the real statues and they were given his approval.

Doyle asked Monk to drive the crates to his office and said he would meet them there shortly. Doyle turned to the appraiser and asked if all was good. The man said all the statues were authentic. Doyle asked him about the value of the articles.

"Well, each statue is valued at least one hundred thousand dollars, so for the nine I'd say just under a million dollars."

Doyle grinned thinking about the recovery fee. He turned to Charles and said, "Make the check out to Doyle Investigations. I can come by tomorrow to get it."

"Worth every penny, Mr. Doyle. The reputation of the gallery is spared the embarrassment of this fiasco. Come by first thing in the morning, I'll have a check for you. Do you have an itemized bill for your services?"

"Just the recovery fee will be more than enough. So don't worry about that."

"Excellent. Thank you again." He turned and went back into the building.

Doyle turned to Monk and thanked him. "After you drop off the crates at my office, stop back by my office later tomorrow, so I can thank you appropriately."

The big man yelled for his men to get into their vehicles and head out. They left. Ferigamo came up to Doyle, "You have some interesting friends."

"They're good to have on your side, believe me. Well, thank you, Len. I hope you worked out the problems of this mess."

"I know what to look for now, thanks."

Doyle said his goodbyes and took Oscar and Poppy out to his car. "Anyone feel like something to eat. I haven't had food since yesterday." They agreed.

At the restaurant, Doyle called Marge. "Did Monk come by with the crates?"

"Yes, Arthur, they are all stacked up in the back. Do you want me to open them and take the statues out?"

"No Marge, they're heavy, wait until we get back." He finished and hung up.

They finished their meal and drove back to the office. Marge was standing by the crates with a hammer in her hand as they came in the door.

"Getting anxious to see them, Marge?" Doyle asked her and took the hammer.

"Of course, I've never seen Egyptian statues close up."

"Well, let's take a look." Doyle went to work opening each crate as Oscar and Poppy pulled the statues out. They put them on a long shelf by Marge's desk along the wall. Marge was flitting from one to another examining them.

"You did get the replicas I presume," Marge asked.

"I presume so, otherwise we may get a visit from the Egyptians," Doyle replied. After all the statues were on display along the wall, Doyle smiled and said, "We have our own little gallery now."

Oscar said, "I'm tired and worn out. I'm going home to rest. See you in the morning." He turned and went out the back door.

"Marge, you may as well go back home. Thanks for coming back here after your ordeal with the intruder."

"I've had so much fun since I've been working here, it's a pleasure." She gathered her things and gave Doyle a quick kiss on the cheek then left, leaving Doyle and Poppy alone with the statues.

"Do you think there may be a curse on any of these?" Poppy asked examining the objects.

"I hope not. It wouldn't be any good for business to have bad luck."

She turned to him and said, "Feel like getting lucky tonight?"

"I don't know, I'm kind of worn too."

"A good rest in bed would be a cure for that," she said with a grin.

He moved closer to her and said, "Your place or mine?"

*

Chapter 26

Doyle was already out of bed before Poppy. He felt invigorated by closing the case and Poppy's acrobatics in bed. They had gone to Doyle's apartment and he was in the shower soaping up when he felt someone move in with him.

"Can't a man take a shower in private," he asked her as she grabbed the soap.

"A girl's got to keep clean, too," she grinned as she ran the soap over his chest and downward.

"Careful, or we'll never get out of here," he said and pulled her arm up.

They towel dried each other, then went to get dressed. Poppy came to him and said, "I'm running home to get a clean change of clothes, then I'll meet you back at your office."

"Works for me." He gave her a kiss and she left the apartment. He finished dressing and went out to his car, driving over to the office. He saw Oscar's car parked in back and went in the building.

Oscar and Marge were standing admiring the statues. "I'm surprised that Charles let you take them," Oscar said.

"I think at the time he was just happy to get the real ones back and avoid an incident with the Egyptians. I don't even think he worried about where these ended up. I like them, so we have our own little exhibit." Doyle went to his desk and picked up the mail, sorting the bills from the junk.

He turned to Oscar and said, "When Poppy gets here, I'm going to collect our fee from the gallery. We'll be set moneywise, now. Think about any new electronic devices we can get to make our work easier."

The back door opened and Poppy came in. Doyle went to her and said, "Ready to go collect money?" She agreed and Doyle yelled to Oscar that he was leaving.

They drove out and over to the gallery. They found Walter Charles in his office, being led by one of the security guards. Doyle thanked the guard as Charles stood.

"Mr. Doyle, thank you for coming. I have your fee ready, and the Egyptians were here bright and early. They were totally unsuspecting of the journey their artifacts took."

Doyle's Quest

"I'm sure you didn't tell them?"

"Of course not. They even offered to bring their King Tut exhibit here. But I will have more security then."

"Good idea," Doyle said as Charles handed him an envelope.

"If you need a reference, please feel free to use us."

"Thanks so much, I'll keep that in mind." They said their goodbyes and Doyle took Poppy back to his car. "Now to the bank," he said.

"Aren't you going to look at it first?" she asked.

Doyle handed her the envelope. She opened it and took out the check. "Oh, pretty. So many zeros," she said with a laugh. Doyle looked at it and whistled.

They went to Doyle's bank and he deposited the check into the firm's account. Then he got four cashier's checks made out. They went back to the car as Doyle signed each check and put them in the envelopes the bank gave him.

He handed one to Poppy. "What's this for?" she asked.

"Your bonus for saving our lives yesterday by shooting Irina and her little friend. Don't spend it all in one place."

"Thank you," she said and looked at the check in the envelope. "Now I can go to Hawaii for the sun."

"Sure, take my money and run." Doyle started the car and drove back to the office. He saw a motorcycle parked by the back door and figured Monk was there.

Inside he found Marge, Oscar and Monk relaxing.

"So is the firm solvent now?" Oscar asked.

"We can order pizzas again," he said and handed an envelope to Monk.

"What's this?" Monk asked.

"A little something so you can throw a huge party for your men," Doyle said. "It's thanks for helping us with the statues. We couldn't have done it without you and your guys."

"Much appreciated, Doyle. Glad to help." He stood and said, "I'll go and get that party started. Join us if you want to. It will probably go on for a few days," he said with a grin and went out the back door.

Doyle's Quest

"Marge, here's a bonus for you that I've been promising for months, and for all you've done for us. Thank you."

"I would have done it for free," she replied.

"Don't make statements that I can use against you." He laughed. "You deserve to get paid for how you put up with us."

He turned to Oscar, and handed him an envelope. "It's now shaping up to be a perfect partnership. I think we deserve some time off. How about going to Hawaii?" Doyle looked at Poppy and grinned.

"I'd rather go to New York," Oscar said. "I have relatives there I haven't seen in a long time."

"Then go where you want. Marge, feel like going to Hawaii?" he asked her.

"I'd love it. Shall I book the reservations?"

"I'll let you know." He took Poppy by the hand and pulled her to the back of the office. "You don't mind if I join you in Hawaii? Or did you have other plans?"

"I was going to ask if you wanted to come. Having Marge along would be fun, too."

"Maybe we could stop in Las Vegas before Hawaii. I've never been there."

"You'd probably blow all your money there. But it's something to think about," she said.

"We have enough money to go anywhere we want."

"Until it runs out and you'd have to come back to chasing cheating spouses."

"We only go around once, so let's enjoy it," he said.

"First, I have to ask you something. Does this make us a couple?"

Doyle paused, then said, "I'm not against it."

"Safe answer. I just don't want to be a fling that you will drop in a week."

He kissed her and said, "I like having you around. You're fun and a bit crazy. Plus you're good with a gun."

"And, I'm good in bed, right?"

"Yes, you are. So, I guess I'll keep you."

Doyle's Quest

"Now, let's make those reservations," she said and pulled him back to the front.

"Marge, pack your bikini, we're going to Hawaii," Doyle said.

Marge busted out laughing and said, "You don't want to see me in a bikini."

*

THE END

~~*~~

Bob Moats

The Jim Richards books by Bob Moats

(In series order)

Classmate Murders
Vegas Showgirl Murders
Dominatrix Murders
Mistress Murders
Bridezilla Murders
Magic Murders
Strip Club Murders
Made-for-TV Murders
Mystery Cruise Murders
Talk Show Murders
Sin City Murders
Black Widow Murders
Vegas Vigilante Murders
Area 51 Murders
Mortuary Murders
Hypnotic Murders
Sunshine State Murders
Blue Suede Murders
Honky Tonk Murders
Dark Carnival Murders
Lipstick Murders
Pasta Murders
Talent Show Murders
Shyster Murders
Campground Murders
Network Murders
Reunion Murders
Big Apple Murders
Kennel Murders
Trick or Treat Murders
Santa Murders
Wiseguy Murders

For a preview or to purchase a book, go to
http://murdernovels.com

Jim Richards Family of Readers

Thanks to the following people who are now part of the Jim Richards Family of Readers. They have read a book or more and enjoyed them. They all volunteered to be included in the list. If you are a fan of the books, send me your full name and you will be included in future books. Send your name to murdernovels@bobmoats.com to be added here and on the website.

* Achim Feifel * Al Norris * Alex Wheatley * Alexandra Delporte-Wilkinson * Amy Tapia * Andrea Bryan * Anne Shepherd * Arianda Sugar * Arlene Markowski * Ashley Augustus * Audra Hall * Barbara Hughes * Barbara Sammons * Barbara Schuler * Barbara Zirger * Beth Donohue Plenskofski * Betsy Childress * Beth Gibson * Bill Sandy * Bill Tornquist * Billie-jo Collie * Boni J Rychener * Candace Larson * Carl Bishopric * Carla Lewis * Carole Henderson * Carolyn Conroy * Carolyn Riddle-Linington * Cassy Bailey * Cathie Turner * Chad Hudson * Charlie Meier * Charlotte L Duran * Cheryl L. Everett * Cindy Ackley Nunn * Cindy Valstad * Connie Bancroft * Corinne Kay O'Daniel * Dana Robbins Chuchran * Dana Wichita * Daniel Kalus * Danielle Monique * Darren Heald * Dave Travers * David Wilkinson * DeAnn Jannereth * Deanna Miller * Deb Breuker Balbo * Debbie Carter * Debbie White * Deborah

Bob Moats

Fartuch * Deborah Gauze * Deborah Sullivan * Dee King * Denise Freeman * Diana Carver * Dixie Beck * Donna Gould * Donna Thompson * Donny Minter * Doris Kight * Eddie Moore * Eric Walters * Felicia Annette Bradfield * Francine Menor * Gail Chesney * Georgiann Minster * George Conner * Greg Colucci * Hayley Rankin * Harold Garcia * Heidi Arnold * Irma Ranee Coy * Jacqueline Moss * Jan Kimball * Jane Lawson * Janice Schneider * Janice Spoor * Jennifer Redmond * Jerry Dornak * Jessica Keown-Belous * Jim Beck * Jo Boguslaw * Jo Turner * Joanne Marie Turner * John Peiffer * John Wisbiski * Joseph Wauro * Joyce Stacy * Joyce Trifiletti * Judy Franklin * Judy Travers * Judy Padgett * Julie Heath * Junnahvee Benson * Karen Dahl * Karen Grams * Karen Higham * Karen Kaiser * Karen Meinburg Richwine * Karen Kirkman Parker * Karin Hawkins * Karin Vasvari * Kathleen Donohue Roesing * Kathleen Riddle-Wolfe * Kathy Hinds Moore * Kathy Jones * Kathy Mitchell * Katie Benzler * Kay Burns * Kelly Garcia * Ken Boggs * Keota Rodriguez * Kiera Mccarthy * Kim Estes * Kitty Stolle * Kristie Sciler * Kirsty Stanton * LaLonnie Scallen * Larry Morris * Leann Parr * Lenora Scales * Leslie Marie Jackson * Linda Forester * Linda Ingle Cox * Linda Kennerö * Linda Magill * Lisa Bower * Lisa Keller * Liz Gibson * Lorraine Wiman * Loretta Alexander * Lynda Bowles * Lynette Lawrance * LuAnn Louttit * Manny Rothman * Marcia Gibson DeWitt * Marie Calder * Marlene Bryan * MaryLouise Kramp * Mary Lynn Gross * Megan Atkins * Meghan Hyden * Melody Cannavan * Michael Carruthers * Michael Dinkens * Michael Vannoy * Michelle Burns-Mitchell * Michelle Pilcher * Micki Potter * Mike Moats * Mimi Baur * Myrna Hecht * Nadine Sutton * Nancy Ellen Sayre * Natalie Quine * Neena Martin * O'Della Wilson * Pat Pollington * Pat Rohn * Patricia Jarmon * Patricia C Trezza * Patrick

Doyle's Quest

Barry * Paul Lawrance * Peggy Davis * Phyllis Bassett * Raylene Matheny * Rebecca Collins Besner * Renee Brumley * Reta Hanna * Reta Moats * Robert Lenski * Roberta Navarro-Harder * Sally Berneathy * Sally Hubler * Sarah Santos * Satka Nikc * Sharon E. Edwards * Sharon Mangini * Sharon McMillon * Sheena Rawl * Sherry Amstutz * Shirley Alvarez * Shirley Davies * Shirley Williams * Stacie Rowe * Stephanie Conner * Steve Cullen * Susan Haughton * Susan Hesse Adams * Susan Salomon * Suzan K Chase * Taisha Cullum * Tamara Moore * Tammy Castleberry * Tammy Lynn Wood * Ted Murphy * Terri Atkins * Terri Creech * Terry Raab * Tonia Rachael Riggs-Williams * Travis Fleury-Lopez * Twyla Gawlas * Val Brooks * Walt Munsel * Yvonne Isakson *

Thank you to all these wonderful people.

Thank you for purchasing this book. I hope you enjoy it as much as I enjoyed writing it for my faithful readers. Please feel free to email me to tell me what you thought about my stories. I love hearing from the readers. I can be reached at murdernovels@bobmoats.com thanks again!

*